I0847513

FABULOUSLY FLAWED

KEENEY BUILDS
BOOK THREE

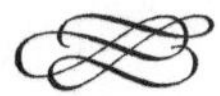

LYNNE HANCOCK PEARSON

ISBN: 979-8-9853527-8-8

Copyright ©2025 Lynne Pearson

Published by All That Editing LLC

All rights reserved. In accordance with the U.S. Copyright Act of 1976, the scanning, uploading, and electronic sharing of any part of this book without the permission of the author is unlawful piracy and theft of the author's intellectual property.

For permissions, contact: lynne@lynnehancockpearson.com

All characters in this book are fictitious. Any resemblance to actual persons, living or dead, is purely coincidental.

This story takes place on the ancestral lands of the Coast Salish. I honor, with gratitude, the land, and its people.

Editing & formatting by: TAFKAM

Cover art by: Designwheelgraphics.com

Visit the author at www.lynnehancockpearson.com

In memory of my mum, Iva Christine Hancock, it has always been an honour to be known as one of the"Iva's girls." And to my sister, Erin Joy Hancock, the favourite of everyone who knew her.

CHAPTER 1

A bottle of bubbly tucked into her tote bag, Sylvie Santiago all but skipped across the parking lot and up the stairs to her apartment. She paused on a step to do a little happy dance.

The bank had approved her mortgage application, and her dream of being a homeowner was close to becoming a reality. Not just a homeowner, either. The property she had her eye on was a duplex that had seen better days. She planned to occupy one side while fixing it up, rent it out, then move into the other side and fix it up. Whether to sell the whole building and move on or keep it and maintain the rental income from one side of the duplex was yet to be determined.

Music blaring from another apartment barely registered as she thought about paint colors. Yellow was her favorite, but should she go with something safer? She'd ask Dean. Sanchez Homes, the premier builder in Keeney, was her boyfriend's family's business. As their marketing specialist, he'd know which colors attracted homebuyers.

Sylvie did a clumsy pirouette as she rounded the corner to her front door, then righted herself. The obnoxious electronic dance music was coming from her apartment. What the hell?

Digging out her keys, she quickened her pace. It was three o'clock on a Monday afternoon. Dean shouldn't be home yet. And he sure as hell shouldn't be playing music that loud.

She pushed the door open, ready to scold him, but the words didn't come out. Takeout containers and empty bottles littered the coffee table, and clothes were strewn all over the floor. The bare backside of a busty blonde bobbed up and down on Dean's spread, naked, hairy thighs.

Sylvie shrieked.

The blonde froze.

Dean poked his head around the woman. "Hey. You're home early."

"Apparently so." Sylvie stomped to the speakers and yanked the cord from the wall. Shock, betrayal, and anger warred inside her. She chose to go with anger. "What the hell, Dean?"

The blonde turned a bleary eye toward Sylvie and slurred, "Who are you?"

Dean patted her backside. "Nobody, babe. Why don't you go get dressed?" He removed her from his lap to reveal his wilting, condom-covered penis. He still wore a polo shirt with the Sanchez Homes company logo on it, and his khakis puddled around his ankles, covering his shoes.

The blonde picked up her scattered clothing, including a black lace bra and panty set that looked suspiciously like one Sylvie owned. Weaving slightly, she pushed a disheveled lock of hair out of her face and, unconcerned with Sylvie's presence, donned the panties and bra.

"Why is she wearing my underwear?" Sylvie demanded, watching the woman try to stuff her ample breasts into bra cups that were much too small for them.

Dean shrugged and reached for a beer. "You never wear

it, so why not?" He leered at the flesh jiggling over the lacy cups. "Besides, it looks better on her."

A weapon. She needed a weapon to scratch his eyes out and cut off his balls. The champagne bottle would have to do. Grabbing it by the neck, she brandished it at Dean and the bimbo.

"Out!" she demanded. "I want you out of my house."

"Chill," he replied. His lack of concern made her wonder if he was high on something. "It's just sex."

"No. It's not *just sex*." Pointing the bottle at the bimbo, she said, "Get dressed and get out. And not in my clothes. But keep the underwear. I don't think I could look at it again."

"And Dean. I want you out. The lease is in *my* name, and this is *my* apartment. I expect you and all your crap to be gone by tomorrow morning."

Tears blurred her vision as she stormed out of the apartment. She was halfway down the hallway when the music started up again.

CHAPTER 2

arl Ryder had *been* to the conference room in Keeney Building Supply, but had never *sat* in the conference room. Never twirled around in a leather chair at the huge table made from reclaimed wood. Never peered through the window over the store's floor, watching shoppers stroll the aisles and peruse products.

KBS had undergone a few changes in the three years he'd been gone. The aisles were wider and the signage above them employed images of products rather than words in English. The *Need Help?* kiosk where homeowners could ask about products or have home improvement questions answered was bigger, now staffed by three Keeney Builds students. It gave him a sense of satisfaction that he'd been involved from the beginning of the program, which provided vocational training for people who struggled to fit into the norm.

Doing so, Carl Ryder felt God-like. That is, until Ali clapped a meaty paw on his shoulder.

"So, the prodigal son has returned?" he boomed.

Before Carl could do more than groan, he was whipped around and seized in a bone-crushing hug.

"Hello, sweetheart," Marcia Ortiz crooned into his ear. "This place hasn't been the same without you."

For the first time in what felt like a decade, Carl's shoulders fell. He breathed deep and sighed, "I missed you, too."

Why did this woman who was older than his mom make him feel like he hung the moon? Like his grandmother, he'd donate a kidney, drive the getaway car, and provide bail money for her. All of that went through his head as Carl melted into her hug, sighing. *Home.*

The words, "Sorry I'm late," jarred him from images of pancakes topped with whipped cream. His eyes popped open to focus on a tiny dynamo of black hair, blacker eyes, lush hips, and a pissed-off aura. All in all, a lethal combination.

He, Ali, and Marcia exchanged wide-eyed glances, watching the woman storm into the room.

"Sylvie?" Marcia's eyebrows came together in a frown. "Are you all right?"

Holy shit! Carl jerked upright. Was this Sylvie Santiago?

She flung a loaded tote bag beneath a stand-up desk and busied herself with the laptop on its surface. "I'm fine."

Marcia released Carl and hurried to her side. "Are you sure? You don't look good."

That was putting it mildly. His memory of Sylvie Santiago was of a woman who smiled big, laughed loud, and sailed through life with confidence. This Sylvie looked... awful. Rumpled clothing that looked like it had been slept in, messy hair in a sloppy ponytail, she was white-faced and vibrating with tension.

Sylvie pressed her lips tightly together. "I'm fine. Really," she snapped.

"If you say so," Marcia replied. "Just, um, let me know if you need anything." She stood with one hand on the edge of the desk and waited. Sylvie stared stonily at her screen, ignoring her.

Head down, Marcia fled the office. Ali shot Sylvie a reproving look before following her.

Carl stared at the doorway, then stared at the woman pounding on her keyboard. "What the hell? That was rude and uncalled for?"

Black eyes scored through him. "Piss off, Carl." And Sylvie Santiago left the room the same way she entered.

❄

*W*ell shit!

She stomped down the corridor searching for Marcia. The nicest, most generous woman she knew, and Sylvie had hurt her feelings.

Ali's small, cluttered office was empty, and no one was in the break room or the bathroom. She clattered down the stairs and burst through the doors leading to the floor, knowing she had to make it right. Taking out her anger, hurt, and frustration on Marcia was wrong.

Other than "I'm sorry," what was she going to say? The truth was too damn embarrassing, but after a sleepless night, she didn't have the bandwidth to come up with a plausible story.

To make matters worse, she'd lost her cool in front of an audience—specifically Carl Ryder. She hadn't seen him in three years, and during that time, he'd filled out in all the best possible ways.

He now wore his hair in tight twists instead of being cropped close, but his eyes still shone, and his smile still blazed against his dark brown skin. He was still long and lean, but his shoulders had broadened, and she'd spotted definition in his arms and legs that hadn't been there when she'd known him. When they'd worked together and joked over lunch breaks and shared the odd beer after work. He'd been cute and quick to smile. Full of energy and dreams.

Those dreams took him away from Keeney to Build Clean, a major construction company in Olympia. Time-wise, it was only two hours away, but the pulse of Washington's capital beat at a faster pace than the sleepy bedroom community, and it was enough of a distance for Sylvie and Carl to lose touch. Despite an attraction she thought was mutual. So, she moved on, dating casually until she met Dean.

Everyone had told her that letting Dean move in with her was moving too fast. Well, not in so many words, but she'd seen the raised eyebrows and shared looks. And ignored them. Dean Sanchez could have had anyone in Keeney—hell, in the Pacific Northwest—and he'd chosen *her*: Sylvie Maria Santiago.

And then screwed her over.

Regardless of how hard she tried, she couldn't scrub away the image of Dean, half-naked and uncaring, and the bimbo in Sylvie's underwear.

Rounding an endcap of plumbing supplies, she slowed, thoughts churning in her over-caffeinated and sleep-deprived mind. How long had Dean been sleeping with her? Was the bimbo the only one? Should Sylvie get tested for STDs?

A sob welled up in her throat as humiliation washed over her. Dean hadn't cared that she knew. His only reaction was to accuse her of overreacting when she told him to be out by morning.

Rubbing a hand against her bruised heart, she choked back her tears and continued her search for Marcia. Her pity party could wait until later.

The confrontation with Sylvie took the shine off his day. Carl stared around at the empty room, then down at the job application form on the conference table. He shook off the uncertainty that tried to creep in. Despite Ali Haddid, the operations manager of KBS, telling him he'd always be welcome back, it was apparent that not everyone felt the same.

He signed his name with a flourish and glanced between the standing desks in the corners of the room. Vincent Ortiz had constructed them, but Carl had helped. He preferred larger building projects, but there was something satisfying about seeing the furniture crafted out of reclaimed wood.

One desk belonged to Vincent's wife. The nameplate resting on it read "Hilary Ortiz, Chief Executive Officer." The nameplate on the other desk had Sylvie's name on it. Carl moved closer to read the sticky note under her name. "Chief Pain in the Ass." He snorted. How appropriate.

Sylvie would probably shred his application, so he left it on Hilary's desk and went back to the window. Near the contractor kiosk, Marcia and Sylvie were holding hands, their heads pressed together. Good. It was weird, he'd never seen that side of Sylvie. But whatever had crawled up her ass, she shouldn't have taken it out on Marcia.

He headed down the stairs and to the main exit, but detoured when Ali waved him over to the Customer Service counter. Like Marcia, he hadn't seemed to have aged a bit. Of course, he was bald, so there was no telling what color his hair was. He was a wee bit paunchier, and as Carl got closer, he realized that Ali now looked up at him, despite standing on a raised platform.

"How long will you be in town?" Ali asked.

Carl leaned against the counter across from him. "Three months." Hopefully, less than that. His parents were engineers working in the Middle East. Their contract would be up about that time, and they would be coming home to release Carl. He gave himself a mental head slap. He shouldn't think of it that way. Caring for his grandmother was *not* a burden.

As if reading his mind, Ali asked, "How is Miss Jean?"

Carl rolled his eyes. "Driving the nursing staff nuts."

His grandmother, Jean Northam, had been a nurse in the days when nurses wore white uniforms, white shoes, and starched caps, and she didn't think much of scrubs and sneakers. She'd fallen and broken a hip and would be released from the rehab center soon. Which was why Carl was back in Keeney. Gram would require care when she returned home, and with his parents overseas and his sister studying for her PhD at Duke University in North Carolina, Carl was given the job.

"I can imagine. What's the plan when she's back on her feet?"

Straightening up, Carl replied, "I head to Alaska to oversee installation of building wrap on a construction project for an oil company."

Ali's bushy eyebrows winged up. "Sounds impressive."

It was. The company he worked for, Build Clean, manufactured and sold building products using environmentally friendly, sustainable materials and practices. A major oil company choosing their products was a big feather in their cap. Carl currently did inside sales and was in the running for a lead position overseeing product installation.

"It's not a done deal, but fingers crossed I beat out the competition." Getting the job in Alaska would send his career skyrocketing.

"It's definitely a done deal. We trained you well," Ali preened.

Carl scoffed, but it was true. He'd interned at KBS and then worked for them as a general contractor for two years. He didn't have an engineering degree from a four-year college, but the collaborative nature of KBS with the Keeney community and the variety of projects he'd worked on made Carl a standout. The coworkers who looked down on him for having gone to a community college or claimed he was a DEI hire could piss off. He twisted around to look over the store.

"Any idea what that was all about?" He jerked his chin toward Marcia and Sylvie, who stood together, Marcia's arm draped around Sylvie's shoulders.

"Not exactly," Ali replied. "A fight with her boyfriend, maybe. Or something like that."

Carl's heart sank a little. If he was going to be stuck in Keeney for a few months, sparring with Sylvie would have been a fun way to pass the time. He put the thought out of his mind to concentrate on the job Ali had for him.

He hadn't swung a hammer or wielded a circular saw in ages, and he was a little nervous. Most of his work at Build Clean was done sitting in front of a computer, and it was rare that he visited a job site.

"Whoa, Tomas. My eyes must be deceiving me because that looks like Carl."

"It can't be. Carl left us for the big city ages ago."

His two former mentors wore big smiles as they crowded him against the counter.

Vincent Ortiz swiped at a nonexistent tear. "Look at our little boy, he's all grown up."

Eyeball to eyeball with the taller of the two men, Carl grinned back. They hadn't changed a bit. On closer inspection, though, there were subtle differences. Stockier than Vincent, Tomas Alvarado no longer wore a perpetual scowl but sported a wedding ring. Not nearly as talkative as Vincent, he was just as painstaking a craftsman. Gram had told Carl that Tomas taught classes on minor home repairs at the senior center, and there was always a waiting list. "Good to have you back. We need another contractor," Tomas said.

"I'm not back for good," Carl replied. "I'm just picking up some work while my grandmother recovers from hip surgery." He wouldn't have to work if Build Clean had approved his request for family leave. Instead, they'd given him an unpaid leave of absence, and he needed to pay rent on his Olympia apartment.

Vincent nodded while he scanned the store. Probably looking for his wife, Hilary.

It was weird seeing the two men look so relaxed and—Carl searched for the right word—domesticated. He knew their original plan was to open their own contracting business, but they'd settled in at KBS. Content to teach classes through the college and senior center, and do renovation projects for homeowners. There was so much more they could have been doing; he didn't know how they weren't bored out of their skulls. His work at Build Clean was so much more fulfilling.

Ali crossed his arms on the counter and said, "There's lots happening around here if you want to stay. Lots of building going on in Keeney."

"Thanks all the same," Carl replied, "but I'm happy in the city." And he was. He liked his apartment. He liked being close to the change-makers in the state capitol. He liked the people he worked with, although it would be nice if the boss wouldn't confuse him with Eric, the other Black guy working at the company.

"You've gotten soft in the city," Vincent said.

"No I haven't." Carl patted his belly. "I practically live at the gym."

"I'm talking about your hands." Vincent held up his own, wiggling the fingers. "The calluses are all gone."

Carl turned his hands over and stared at his palms. There was an old scar across the base of one thumb, but they were otherwise smooth. "And that's a bad thing?"

Vincent winked. "Chicks dig calluses. Didn't you know that?"

"So that's why I can't get a date," Carl replied mournfully. The truth was, he rarely tried. The women he met were fine, but there was no one who'd made him look twice.

Their heads all turned at the sound of laughter. Four women stood in the middle of an aisle: Marcia, Hilary, Tomas's wife, Fiona, and Sylvie. Marcia was gesturing wildly to the amusement of the others.

Tomas and Vincent shook their heads while Ali grinned. "Yeah," he said. "You might be happy in the city, but there's a lot to be said for small towns. You can do a lot of living here."

The three men wandered over to the women, who made room for them, smiling and laughing the whole time.

As a condition of letting him take a leave of absence, Carl's boss, Scott, asked him to reach out to a property developer in Keeney. Build Clean was interested in expanding into residential construction, and the company was making a name for itself.

While marketing wasn't his area of expertise, Carl believed that Clean Wrap was a superior product to its competition. If talking it up would get him closer to the Alaska job, he was willing to do so.

Carl sipped his water and looked over his talking points while waiting for the guy to join him at the busy sushi restaurant on Main Street.

"Carl Ryder?"

He looked up to see a good-looking man in his mid-thirties smiling at him.

"That's me." He stood and held out his hand.

"Dean Sanchez. Nice to meet you." He shook hands and sat across from Carl, waving over a server.

They placed their orders, and Dean followed the server

with his eyes as she retreated. He turned back, waggling his eyebrows and smirking. "Too bad that's not on the menu."

Carl made a noncommittal sound and took a drink of water.

"So, you're with Build Clean."

"I am."

"And you're here to woo me." He clasped his hands against his chest. "I feel so special."

Carl's laugh made Dean smile, and the two men settled into an enjoyable conversation about building wraps, baseball, and skiing versus snowboarding.

At least ten years older than Carl, Dean Sanchez was smart and charming, and if Carl were interested in men, he'd definitely want his number.

They swapped business cards at the end of the meal, and Dean said, "You've sold me, but I have to talk to the old man. Sometimes he's of the 'if it ain't broke, don't fix it' mindset."

"I hear you," Carl replied. It was hard for companies to try new products when they perceived nothing wrong with what they were using. "Let me know if I can do a demonstration for the company. That might sway him."

Dean bobbed his head. "Maybe. Truth is, I'm going to be branching out on my own. Just getting my funding in place before I make my move. Not new construction, though. Don't want to compete directly with the old man."

"So, renos then?" That would be competition for KBS contractors. The idea gave Carl a stab of guilt, as if he were conspiring with the enemy.

"Nope. I'm going to buy older homes, bring them up to date, then sell them. Easy money. Maybe start a YouTube channel. Do you think people will subscribe to watch me swing a hammer?" He flexed, making his biceps pop.

Carl laughed. "I'm sure you'd do just fine."

They parted ways outside the restaurant, and Carl leaned against a wall to email his boss. Build Clean may not get a contract with Sanchez Homes, but Carl had established a relationship with someone who was undoubtedly a major player in the building community.

❄

Sylvie had apologized profusely to Marcia by telling her—with many tears and expletives thrown in—about her split with Dean. In turn, Marcia shared that her ex-husband had had a roving eye. They'd divorced when Vincent was young, and the experience had made her reluctant to get serious with another man.

Crying always gave Sylvie a headache, and it lingered well into midday, despite her determination to work through it. A slight throb hovered behind her sinuses when a call came in around two o'clock.

"Keeney Building Supply," she answered. "How may I help you?"

"Umm…may I speak to Sylvie Santiago?"

Only then did she register that she'd answered her cellphone and not the office line.

"This is she."

"Ms. Santiago, this is Arthur Finkel, the property manager of Keeney Commons. I'm calling to inform you that you have been evicted and have forty-eight hours to be out of your apartment."

Her knees buckled, and she collapsed into her chair. "Evicted? No! There must be a mistake."

"No, Ms. Santiago," he said sharply. "This was the third strike. I warned you."

"You did not warn me, and I have no idea what you're talking about."

A beleaguered sigh came through the phone. "Ms. Santiago, I spoke directly to your partner about the offensive music. *Twice*. And gave him a written notice. *Twice*. The terms are in the lease agreement that you signed. Quiet hours are between ten pm and seven am. Last night was the third complaint against you."

"But I never received them. Dean never gave them to me!"

"That may well be, but notices were delivered to you, emailed to you, and are archived in the online portal. If *you* failed to read them, that's your problem."

He went on about her needing to be out in forty-eight hours and that the apartment needed to be cleaned, but Sylvie didn't hear him. Her headache had taken on new life, threatening to burst through her eye sockets. She hung up the phone and lowered her head to the desk. "Fuck my life," she mumbled.

"What was that, dear?"

Sylvie whipped her head up to see Iris McLeod, the owner of KBS, standing in the doorway. The bird-like woman had given over the running of KBS to Hilary and now worked as an assistant to Fiona. Divorced from Iris's son Eddie, Fiona was the executive director of Keeney Works and was married to Sylvie's half-brother, Tomas Alvarado. Sylvie joked to friends that she needed a flow chart to explain the relationship between Keeney Building Supply, Keeney Works, and Keeney Builds.

"Just—" Sylvie flapped her hand at the cluttered surface of her desk. "It's nothing."

"Does it have anything to do with Dean?" Iris scrunched up her face. "Sorry, dear. Marcia told me you had a falling-out."

Falling out. That polite, old-fashioned term didn't begin to explain it. Iris waited patiently while Sylvie considered what to say. There wasn't much point in hiding things. Keeney was a small town, and word about her eviction would eventually get out. Thank God her parents were on vacation. She had some time to get settled before they returned.

"I've been evicted." Iris gasped at the bald statement but didn't say anything as Sylvie explained.

While Iris made sympathetic noises, Sylvie opened up the tenant portal for Keeney Commons and found the violation notices. Both incidents occurred within the past month and included timestamps.

Thinking about the dates and times, she realized they'd happened when she had been working late at her other job—mudding and taping drywall for new home construction. It was a lucrative side business that padded her bank account but crimped her social life. A fact that Dean had complained about. Often. Had he been boffing the blonde both nights as well? Bile rose at the image of Dean having sex with someone in her bed.

"Well, I hate to say you're in luck, because I'm sure you don't feel lucky," Iris said. "But my rental suite is available. It's been empty for a few months, just waiting for the perfect tenant."

It would have been nice to be able to say "No, thank you. I've got this." But she didn't. Sylvie was adrift in a leaky boat that was taking on water, so she grasped at the lifeline. "Thank you!" she cried, leaping out of her chair to hug her boss.

"Oh, poo. It's nothing." Iris pulled a crumpled tissue from her sleeve and handed it to Sylvie. "Best practices would dictate that I have you fill out an application and provide references. And that I do a background check on you. But you work for me. I go to church with your mother. And my former daughter-in-law is your sister-in-law. Now, let's arrange to get you moved."

CHAPTER 3

The nice thing about staying in his grandmother's house was that Carl could drink his first cup of coffee in his underwear. Her programmable coffeemaker was older than he was, and remembering her instructions, he'd set the machine up the night before. When his alarm went off, he was greeted with the mouthwatering aroma. Blinking sleepily, he sipped the dark brew and scratched absently at his belly.

Other than the ticking wall clock and the hum of the refrigerator, the house, a three-bedroom rancher at the end of a cul-de-sac, was quiet. Built in the 1970s, his grandparents were the original owners, and while it was clean and in good shape, the furnishings were dated because Gram didn't believe in replacing something simply because it was out of style. He pulled out a chair at the Formica-topped table and stared out the sliding glass door at the backyard, noting that the grass needed cutting. He picked up his phone to jot that down on the to-do list that seemed to get longer and longer.

A text came in from Ali: *Change of plans. Be here by 8 and stretch first. Lots of heavy lifting today.*

That was fine by Carl. He'd spent the previous day following Ali around KBS like a brand new hire. After three years away, he understood why it was necessary, but it was boring as hell, and it seemed like half of Keeney came through the doors. They all wanted to talk to him, inquiring about his work with Build Clean (apparently, Gram had told everyone she knew about what he did) and asking for updates on Gram. While he knew they were simply being friendly, he wasn't used to the attention. Hell, he didn't even know the names of his next-door neighbors in his apartment building in Olympia. And he liked it that way.

The address Ali sent him was unfamiliar. Though a small town, Keeney was growing like every other community within an hour's commute of Seattle. It had good schools, a responsive city council, lots of green space, and a reputation for being inclusive and neighborly. And thank God for that. It was a neighbor who'd seen his grandmother go down and called 911 to get her to the hospital. No doubt they'd help out when she returned home, which was a good thing because Gram would still need some assistance after he left.

Carl acknowledged Ali's text, got dressed, and headed out the door.

His GPS led him to the Keeney Commons apartment complex, and he spotted a KBS truck backed up to a curb. Ali stood at the back of the truck, surrounded by people Carl didn't recognize but assumed were Keeney Builds students. Grabbing his travel mug, he walked over to join them.

"Good." Ali greeted Carl with a nod and addressed the others. "Everyone's here, and we can get started. We start with the furniture and then load the boxes. They should be well-packed, but handle them with care. Marcia will have my head if anything gets broken. Rex and Daveed, when the apartment is empty, you are the cleaning crew. Iris will give you the supplies and instructions. Scour that place until it shines and don't dilly-dally. We only have today to do everything."

As Ali continued delivering instructions, Carl's gaze traveled over the well-maintained buildings, wondering who was in a bind and had to move in a hurry. His job was to dismantle the bed and anything else that needed to be taken apart before being moved. Ali gave him a toolbox, and he hung back while watching the others file up the stairs and toward the open door at the end of the corridor.

"You've got four students hauling boxes and cleaning. Is that really the best use of their time, or is KBS going into the moving business?" Carl asked.

Ali shot him a cool look. "I don't know about the company you've been working for, but at KBS, when a friend needs help, we're there. If that's not something you're willing to do, I'll see you tomorrow."

Thoroughly put in his place, Carl climbed the stairs and got into line behind the others. Standing beside an open door, Sylvie greeted each person with a smile and a word of thanks before her gaze met his. The smile wavered then firmed up. Red spots dotted her cheeks, though she held her head high. "Morning, Carl." Radiating with thinly veiled tension, she whipped around before he could respond, and he stared after her, his eyes fixed on the swinging ponytail as she disappeared from sight.

Being a smart-ass was second nature to Carl, but after Ali's remarks and seeing the way Iris and Marcia treated Sylvie with kid gloves, he kept his comments to himself. Instead, he worked swiftly and efficiently, taking apart the dining table and media stand before heading to the bedroom. Daveed carried away the boxed-up bedding, and Carl muscled the mattress aside to prop it against the wall. A balled-up piece of neon green lay squished on top of the box spring.

He picked it up without thinking.

"Hey, could you—" With Marcia right behind her, Sylvie stood in the doorway, mouth hanging open, and her face drained of color. Her gaze was fixed on Carl's hand. More specifically, the fabric.

His cheeks flamed as he realized he was holding a pair of women's panties.

Sylvie left without saying another word.

"I don't think those are hers," Marcia said, plucking the offending fabric out of his hand before leaving the room.

"Oh." He stared stupidly at the empty doorway, then back at the box spring. Taking a utility knife from his back pocket, he proceeded to methodically slash the fabric covering the box spring and mattress. Marcia returned to find him shoving the knife back into his pocket.

"Oops," he said blandly. "I tripped. Guess I'll have to replace the bed."

Marcia's lips twitched. "Guess so," she replied, equally as blandly.

❄

*W*atching Arthur Finkel go through the apartment like a white-gloved health inspector had been humiliating. Sylvie stuck out her tongue at his retreating back and pulled out of the parking lot of Keeney Commons for the last time, blessing the big hearts and organizational skills of Marcia, Ali, and Iris. Due to their diligence and the team of KBS workers, the windows sparkled, the appliances gleamed, and there wasn't a speck of dust in the place. Despite the circumstances, a pang went through her as the buildings disappeared from sight. While Tomas had originally lived there, she had taken over the lease on her own merit, slowly replacing her brother's cast-offs with furniture specifically chosen for her first grown-up home. It wouldn't be the same, but she would make the items work in the new place.

The sun was beginning to set over the stately firs that lined the long driveway of Iris's home as Sylvie drove down the quiet street.

Vincent Ortiz had converted the two-story house into two apartments after Iris's husband passed away. He'd also retrofitted the old backyard garden shed into a tiny house that was currently occupied by a young seminary student interning at Keeney United Methodist Church.

Sylvie was getting a skookum deal on rent and suspected Iris was doing the same for the student.

The driver for a delivery service climbed into the cab of his truck as Sylvie drove up the driveway. She pulled to the side to allow him to pass and then parked in the empty space. Getting out of her car, she waved at Marcia, who was bundling cardboard and plastic wrap into the recycle bin.

"What's that?" Sylvie asked. She'd accepted Marcia's assistance with arranging the furniture but declined her offer to help her unpack. Instead, she'd told Ali and his crew to stack boxes in one of the three bedrooms, allowing her the leisure to take her time figuring out where to put things.

Carl and Ali descended the stairs and joined them before Marcia could answer. Sylvie didn't mind the presence of Ali and Marcia; they were like family, only better. They showered her with affection and never made her feel like she was being interrogated.

Her last interaction with Carl had been less than friendly, yet today, he'd worked harder than anyone. Not talking, simply doing whatever was required, whether someone asked him or not. She hadn't expected that from him, nor had she expected him to still be here.

"So, um, about your bed." Ali ran a hand over his bald head and looked at Marcia, who in turn looked at Carl.

A bead of sweat trickled down his dark, handsome face,

and he rubbed his jaw against his shoulder. "One of the guys tripped and spilled something on your bed."

Sylvie shrugged. "Okay. I can clean it." She'd planned on dousing it in bleach anyway.

"That's not gonna work," Marcia blurted.

"Why not?"

The three exchanged wide-eyed looks.

"Because it was—" Carl looked everywhere but at her "—a milkshake. Strawberry milkshake! And the kid didn't tell us about it until after the stain had set, and it smelled to high heaven, so we got you a new one."

Ali bobbed his head, and Marcia said, "Consider it a housewarming present."

They were terrible liars, but she didn't press them on it because she wouldn't have been able to sleep in the old bed anyway. Somehow she'd have to make it up to this group of selfless individuals who'd rallied around her, no questions asked. She flung herself at Ali and Marcia, hugging them tightly. "I don't deserve you guys. Thank you so much!"

Turning to Carl, she hesitated.

Disappointment flashed across his face before he grinned and held his hands up. "I'm sweaty and disgusting, a hearty thank you will do just fine."

"No, it won't." She pushed his hands aside and went in for what was supposed to be a brief hug.

Carl's arms wrapped around her, and he squeezed, resting his chin on the top of her head.

"Anytime," he murmured. "Anytime."

*A*fter they left, she ordered a pizza and hopped in the shower to wash off the sweat and stress of the day. While getting dressed afterward, she mulled over the idea of hosting a barbecue for everyone who'd helped out. The suite had a beautiful deck with furniture that had been crafted by

Iris's husband. Beer, soft drinks, and takeout from her parents' restaurant would be easy. And she'd ask Iris if they could play bocce in the backyard. A knock sounded, startling her out of party planning mode.

Clutching a cardigan tightly around her, Iris stood on the other side of the French doors.

"Hey," Sylvie said, opening the door. "Your timing is perfect. The pizza is still hot. Want some?"

"Thank you, dear, but I won't bother you."

Sylvie waved her off. "It's no bother at all. I will happily share a pizza with you every day for the rest of your life to thank you."

"That's sweet," Iris mumbled.

Something was off. Sylvie wiped her hands on a paper towel and faced her new landlady. "What's up?"

Iris looked everywhere but at her before finally blurting, "Your check bounced."

"That's not possible." And it wasn't. The check was drawn on an account with a balance of more than $300,000. She'd won the money at a Mariners' 50/50 raffle a few months back and had augmented that amount with the mudding and taping jobs she did on the side.

"It did," Iris said. "I'm so sorry."

"Hang on, there's been a mistake." Sylvie whipped out her phone and opened her banking app only to discover the system was down for maintenance. Showing the message to Iris, she said, "I know it's a mistake, and I'll go to the bank tomorrow to fix it. I can bring you cash if you'd prefer."

"That's not necessary," Iris replied, looking even more embarrassed than Sylvie felt. "I know you're good for it, and I'm sorry. I should have waited until tomorrow to tell you."

"No, no. There's nothing to apologize for. I'm glad you told me now so I can take care of it first thing in the morning."

"All right. Can I help you unpack?"

Sylvie blinked back tears at Iris's unflinching generosity and gave her landlady/employer a hug before leading her to the door. "Thank you, but I think I'm going to bed soon. I'm dead on my feet and can barely keep my eyes open."

Wide awake at three o'clock, Sylvie crawled out of the unfamiliar bed in the unfamiliar room, wishing Iris had waited to tell her about the bounced check. The number of people in Keeney who knew about her nest egg was small. It included her immediate family, Marcia, Ali, and Iris, and, well, anyone who'd seen her image on the jumbotron at the baseball game, including Dean.

Armed with a cup of coffee, Sylvie put away the bath products from the box she'd opened and left on the counter the night before, her mind churning like a hamster wheel. Dean knew about the money and knew about her plans. And supported them. They'd driven around Keeney looking at possible houses to flip and even sketched out preliminary budgets. Although, she thought while staring at a box of tampons, his enthusiasm had waned lately. He'd found fault with the duplex she wanted and scoffed at her design ideas, telling her not to be so hasty.

She'd refreshed the banking app multiple times during the night but was still getting the same message that the system was down, and unease churned in her gut. There was nothing she could do until the bank opened, and she needed something to keep herself busy. About to break down the empty box and take it to the recycling, she wondered if she was being too hasty.

What if the money was truly gone?

What if Iris evicted her?

What if Iris evicted and *fired* her?

Sylvie stared at her wild-eyed image. "Give your head a shake," she muttered. She had been told more than once that she had a tendency to jump to conclusions. Really, the worst that would happen was that she'd have to tell her parents and move back home.

Deciding to refresh her nail polish, she cued up a YouTube video of someone pressure washing their back deck and zoned out while painting her toes a perky pink.

CHAPTER 4

A bank employee finally unlocked the door at nine o'clock, and Sylvie rushed inside. The tellers eyed her uneasily, one or maybe both of them, with their hands on the panic button. Sylvie painted on a smile, slowed her pace, and tried to slow her heart rate.

"Good morning," she chirped, the words coming out louder than intended. She lowered her voice and went on, "I'd like a cashier's check, please. And could you please tell me the balance in my account? Your system is down, and I can't access it."

The young teller's stiff stance relaxed, and she pushed her glasses up her nose. "Certainly, ma'am. May I see your ID?"

"Right. Sorry about that." Sylvie proffered her driver's license with a shaky hand. She had way too much caffeine in her system and was jittery all over.

Bernice Kwan, according to the teller's name tag, clicked a few keys, scratched a few numbers onto a piece of paper, and slid it across the counter.

"That's not possible," Sylvie said for the second time in less than twenty-four hours. "That account" —she stabbed her finger at one number— "should have close to three hundred and twenty thousand dollars in it." The other bank balance, while considerably lower, seemed accurate. It was the one she used for regular expenses. "Please check again," she said.

"It's not a mistake," Bernice replied. She twisted the monitor and gestured for Sylvie to see for herself.

Standing on tiptoes, Sylvie craned her neck and peered at the screen. Fear and dismay engulfed her. The nest egg that she'd been nurturing had a balance of $729.00.

"Hi Sylvie, is there something wrong?"

Sylvie twisted and gaped at the bank manager. Andrea Marquez and her family lived next door to Sylvie's parents and had opened the account for Sylvie when she'd received the check from the Mariners organization.

"My money. It's all gone," Sylvie said.

"I'm sure there's an explanation. Let's go into my office." She indicated a glass-walled room off to the side. "Bernice, please run a transaction report and bring it to me."

Sylvie followed Andrea and plopped into a faux-leather chair facing a desk.

"It will just take a moment," Andrea said. She was a plump, pleasant-faced woman in her early fifties. Photos of her now-college-age twin boys adorned the credenza behind her. They'd been little hellions when Sylvie used to babysit them, always trying to sneak Game Boys into their rooms after bedtime.

Coming in to drop the printout on Andrea's desk, Bernice darted a sympathetic look at Sylvie and quickly left. The look didn't bode well.

Andrea studied the report with pursed lips. "It looks like there have been a number of transfers out of the account, starting about a month ago."

Sylvie shook her head and tried to keep calm. "No. I put

money into that account and have never taken anything out of it. May I?" Andrea gave her the report, and Sylvie looked over the transactions. All the transfers, in varying amounts, were deposited into the same account number. She tapped the paper. "I don't know who this account belongs to, and I didn't make these transfers."

"Does anyone else have access to this account? "Andrea asked, her fingers flying over the laptop keyboard.

"No. You should know. You set up the account for me."

Andrea gave her a bland look. "I did. But that doesn't mean *you* haven't allowed someone access to your account."

"But I haven't!" Sylvie's voice rose along with her panic. "I've never given out my password. Do you think it's identity theft?"

"It's possible," Andrea said grimly. "But let's do a little more digging." She clicked on some more keys and turned to retrieve a printout from the small printer behind her. "Someone *does* have access to your account."

Sylvie took the paper and studied it. On the line below her name, Dean Sanchez was listed.

"Is that your signature?"

"Yes. But I don't know how that could be. I didn't come in with Dean to sign this. I'd remember that."

Andrea looked even grimmer. She picked up the phone and requested that someone bring her the original paperwork.

A few minutes later, a woman breezed into the room. About the same age as Sylvie, she was immaculately made up and dressed in a power red suit with shoes to match. She smiled perfunctorily at Sylvie, handed over the document, and turned for the door.

Andrea stopped her. "Hang on, Ingrid, and close the door."

Then she turned her serious gaze on Sylvie. "Look closely and tell me if you remember signing this."

Thinking it was pointless, Sylvie scanned the document and was about to give it back when she stopped. On the back side of the paper was a small scribble in the upper left-hand corner, something she always did to make sure a pen's ink flowed well. She closed her eyes and thought carefully, trying to bring the memory into focus. "I did sign this," she said. "But not here in the bank. My boy—former boyfriend, and I were planning to flip a house together, and he gave me a bunch of papers to sign in preparation for forming a company."

She pointed at the scribble. "I always test the pen before I sign my name so my signature is legible." She shifted her gaze between Andrea and the other woman, Ingrid. "A habit I picked up from an old boss."

"I see," Andrea said, but she wasn't looking at Sylvie. "Was anyone else there when you signed the papers?"

"No," Sylvie replied, twisting in her chair to follow Andrea's gaze. There was something oddly familiar about Ingrid, but she couldn't place her. The blonde woman was staring down at the carpet, no longer looking like a polished professional.

Andrea's voice was steely. "Ingrid, your initials are on this document as the witnessing officer. Care to explain?"

An unbecoming purple stained the blonde's cheeks. "Dean—that is, Mr. Sanchez came in asking to be added to the account. When I explained that the account holder had to be present, he asked if he could take the paperwork with him to speed up the process."

"That is against the bank's policy."

Beads of sweat now stood out on Ingrid's forehead as she nodded. "Yes, I know, but I figured there wouldn't be any harm in it because he said that the account holder would be coming back with him."

Andrea's raised hand prevented Sylvie from protesting. "And then what happened?"

"Mr. Sanchez came back by himself because his sister" — Ingrid glanced at Sylvie— "was sick. But he brought a photocopy of her driver's license to prove it was her signature." Her head bobbed so hard a lock of hair fell over her forehead, hiding her eyes. She pushed it aside with the back of her hand.

Sylvie gasped. "You! You were the one schtupping Dean."

"I was not," Ingrid snapped. "Wait, what does schtupping mean?"

"It means having sex. Precisely what you were doing with *my* boyfriend on *my* couch." Sylvie leaped out of her chair and backed the blonde into a corner, angrier than she'd ever been in her life. "How long have you been banging Dean? Was it your idea or his to go after my money? What did—" An arm banded around her waist and drew her back.

"Stop that," Andrea hissed, forcing Sylvie into a chair. Yanking the door open, she pointed to the bank's lobby, where tellers and customers gawked at them. "Ingrid, go into your office and stay there. I will deal with you later."

She closed the door and heaved a great sigh. "Syl—"

"I know, I know, I'm sorry. I shouldn't have lost control."

"That may be," Andrea replied, returning to sit in her chair. "But it was perfectly understandable. I'll start an investigation to see about getting your money back."

"An investigation?"

"Yes. I can, and will terminate Ingrid. However, if she and Dean Sanchez are in a relationship, and she attests to witnessing you sign that document, even if it wasn't in the bank, it will be a matter of his word against yours." She waited a beat before adding, "You may want to talk to a lawyer."

Unable to speak, Sylvie nodded and left Andrea's office. Keeping her head down, she scuttled to the entrance, only looking up when a pair of polished men's loafers came into view. "Oh. Good morning, Mr. Sanchez."

Ron Sanchez, Dean's father, was a silver fox and a total sweetheart. "Sylvie, it's so nice to see you." His smile faded slightly, but his eyes were still warm as he said, "I'm sorry you and Dean broke up. You take care now. " He patted her arm awkwardly before stepping aside to allow her to exit.

❄

*W*aiting in the truck for Ali to return with the "best bagels in the state," Carl scrolled mindlessly through his phone. Although he was not receiving a paycheck, he remained an employee of Build Clean and had access to the company's Slack channel. He noted the ongoing debate about wind power versus solar panels, the updates to the hockey pool, and the stats for the company softball team. And sighed. Someone had posted, "Sure could have used Ryder as shortstop. McKay sucks."

That was it. The only thing the company missed about Carl was his ability to catch a ball. It wouldn't be long before he'd be back there to refresh their memory about his contracting skills. They were better than his fielding skills.

He tossed his phone aside and rolled his shoulders. Despite being twenty-four and in decent shape, hauling Sylvie's furniture around had taken its toll, and he wondered about the guy who'd stepped out on her. He had to be a moron. Sylvie Santiago was a firecracker.

But she'd had little spark yesterday. Barely a fizzle. Hopefully, sleeping in a bed that had been unsullied by another woman's presence would help. When she'd hugged him last night, tucking her head under his chin, she'd fit perfectly, and Carl hadn't wanted to let go, wanted her to know his arms were a safe place. It wasn't how he'd envisioned holding her for the first time, but he was glad to have given her something good at the end of what must have been a shitty few days.

Bang!

He craned his neck to see where the noise was coming from. Across the street, Sylvie was kicking the shit out of a car door.

"You asswipe!" she yelled at the person inside. Apparently, she'd gotten her spark back.

A guy in a ballcap scrambled over the console and into the driver's seat and out the opposite door. "Babe," he called, rounding the hood and holding his hands up. "Stop that."

Sylvie glared at him. "You lost the right to call me 'babe' when you decided to screw that bimbo. And now you've taken my money?" She aimed another kick at the car, but the guy clamped his arms around her and pulled her away.

Carl opened the truck door, ready to intervene. However, it wasn't necessary. Sylvie shook the much bigger guy off with little effort. Carl got out of the truck anyway.

"What's going on?" Ali asked. He put a paper bag on the hood of the truck and handed Carl a coffee.

"Sylvie's reaming out her old boyfriend. Do you know who that is?"

Ali sipped his coffee and squinted at the guy. "Yeah, Dean Sanchez. He's the presumptive heir to Sanchez Homes. You don't know him?"

Carl froze, then nodded slowly. "I know the name." The charming guy he'd had lunch with? The guy who'd just invited him to a Mariners game? Who had seats in the Diamond Club section? That was the guy who'd screwed around on Sylvie? Carl's life had just gotten more complicated. In a tight voice, he said, "Sylvie just accused him of taking her money."

"That's not good." Ali munched on a bagel, watching the interaction.

"Do you know anything?"

Ali shushed him and pointed.

"I didn't take your money," Dean said. "I transferred it to the business account."

"Bullshit. You scammed me into signing my name and took my money."

Dean made a face. "That's not the way I remember it. You knew what you were signing."

Dammit! Two passing cars blocked Sylvie and Dean from view. When they were gone, Sylvie was alone, looking bewildered and dejected. She swiped under her eyes and trudged down the sidewalk.

Bites of bagel turned to sawdust in Carl's mouth. When he'd left her last night, she'd been tired but happy. Now she looked like the weight of the world had settled on her shoulders. "Should we check on her?"

"Nope."

"Seriously? She's a mess and she's—"

"And she'd be mortified to know we saw that." Ali grabbed the rest of the bagels. "Hop in the truck, we've got a job to get to. I'll get Marcia to check in on Sylvie."

Carl stared after Sylvie's retreating form, not feeling good about leaving her there and feeling worse about his dealings with Dean. But maybe Ali was right. What could he do anyway? The question churned in his head the rest of the morning.

*A*li Haddid knew everyone in Keeney. At least, it seemed that way to Carl. Ali told stories about the businesses they passed and the people he waved to, and caught Carl up on all the goings-on in town. Including that Sanchez Homes would be building twenty houses in a new community outside of town. It was the opening Carl was looking for.

He learned about Sylvie and her sister winning the money, her plans to flip houses, and her side business mudding and taping. And he learned that she'd been over the moon with Dean Sanchez. Ali seemed pleased that they'd broken up.

"Don't get me wrong," he said. "It tears me up to see Sylvie heartbroken. I knew he wasn't right for her even before he screwed around on her."

"Yeah? Why?"

They were taking measurements to redo a powder room, and he was on the floor with a tape measure, while Ali leaned against the door jamb, watching him.

Ali's eyebrows beetled together, and he blew out a breath. "How do I explain this? In Keeney's social hierarchy, Sylvie's parents are up there. And it's not because they care about status. The Santiagos are smart businesspeople—Louisa runs the restaurant and food truck while Carlos runs Woodbine Automotive—and active church members. They care about what happens in Keeney, and the community respects them a lot."

"Not so with the Sanchezes?"

"It's a little more complicated than that. The family moved here about ten years ago, and Ron's company has been building homes all over Keeney. The houses are good, well-made, but pricey. Sanchez Homes gets their supplies from a variety of places, and there's a lot of competition for their business. But Ron doesn't play favorites. He does the same thing with his personal wealth. He supports many organizations, but not in a flashy way. He's careful."

"Calculating?" Carl rose to his feet and dusted off his knees.

"Umm, not necessarily," Ali replied. "He knows it's good business to give back, but I don't think he cares about anything in particular. And the same applies to his son."

The measurements done, they spoke to the homeowner about the next steps and headed back to the truck. While Ali drove, Carl went back to their conversation.

"Do you think Dean didn't care for Sylvie?" he asked.

"I think he's flashy, and I think he's a user. I think he got what he wanted from Sylvie and decided to move on."

Carl squinted against the afternoon sunshine. Thinking of schmoozing Dean to get the Sanchez Homes account while interacting with Sylvie at KBS was giving him a headache. He was going to have to be very, very careful.

CHAPTER 5

is grandmother lay in bed, eyes closed, looking drawn. Her usually glossy dark complexion was ashen, and the silk scarf tied around her head drooped to the side. She looked…old. And frail. The thought that she might not completely recover entered his head for the first time. And scared the shit out of him. With his parents overseas and his sister on the other side of the country, Gram was his anchor.

Someone tapped him on the arm, and he turned to find the director of the rehab facility.

"Mr. Ryder?" she inquired. "May I speak to you for a moment?"

Carl glanced at his grandmother's sleeping form and nodded. He followed the woman down a hallway lined with rooms filled with patients in varying stages of recovery.

"I'm Debra Anderson, the director here," the woman said, leading him into an office that was comfortable but cluttered, and gesturing him to a chair.

"Nice to meet you. Is my grandmother doing okay?"

Her answering smile was not reassuring. "Okay? Yes. As well as we'd like? No."

His knee started to bob. "What does that mean?"

"It means that we don't think she should live by herself."

The frank statement caught him off guard. "But I thought…" he didn't know what he thought. That Gram would bounce back with little effort. That she'd be home in a few weeks and bustling around her house like she had for decades. "So, she needs someone to check in on her a few times a day? Like someone from her church? I can put railings in the bathroom and widen the doorways if she needs a walker."

The rehab director eyed him sympathetically but shook her head. "I'm afraid that won't be enough. Full-time care is our recommendation." Finding a folder on her desk, she pulled out a form. "Fortunately, Miss Jean is as sharp as a tack and anticipated this kind of situation. She put herself on the waiting list for Cascades Lodge a few years back."

He gaped. "She's going into the home?"

"Not exactly. Cascades Lodge offers various levels of care, starting with assisted living, which is what your grandmother requires. She'd have her own apartment and could choose between making her own meals or eating in the dining room with the other residents. When she declines," the director met his gaze directly, "and needs higher levels of care, she'll move into a room on a floor with twenty-four-hour nursing care. And that will remain her room."

Until she dies.

Seeing he'd grasped her unfinished sentence, the director sat back in her chair.

"My grandmother—" Carl cleared his throat. "She made all these arrangements?"

"She did. And she knows the time to transition to assisted living is now."

Carl stared dumbly at her desk, noticing the neat pile of folders and wondering how many similar conversations the director would be having that day.

As if she were on the same wavelength, she stood and handed Carl a business card, saying, "I've already contacted Cascades and they anticipate having an assisted living unit ready in a week or so."

"Does Gram know that, too?" Carl asked, rising from the chair on shaky legs.

"Yes. I believe she's started a list for you."

Carl snorted. "No doubt she has."

The director handed him another business card. "This process can be overwhelming, and this is the number of a woman who assists families transition their loved ones."

Carl accepted the card. *Process* and *transition* were such benign words for "they're never going to get better."

Thanking the director, he headed out the front door to gulp in a big breath. Shit, that happened fast. Gram wouldn't be coming home all because of a broken hip? A parade of his best memories passed before him, most featuring his grandmother, and many of them at the Formica-topped table in her house. The house that she would need to move out of and eventually sell. Overwhelmed and more than a little frustrated, he pulled out his phone and stabbed at the keys, not caring that it was the middle of the night in Kuwait.

His father picked up almost right away. "Hey, is everything okay?"

"No, Dad, no, it's not."

"Hang on, I'm putting you on speaker."

His mom came on the line, more than a trace of impatience in her voice. "What is it, Carl? What's wrong?"

"Gram won't be coming home. The rehab director says she needs to go into assisted living."

"Ahh," his mother said. "So it's time then."

He pulled the phone away from his ear and stared at it. "What do you mean 'it's time?'" There was a rustling noise as he heard his parents shuffle around.

"Your grandmother is eighty-two, has high blood

pressure, and congestive heart failure. We knew this day would come." Monica Ryder did not mince words. She never had. Times like this, Carl wished his mother would. "I know she's made preparations, so check in with her, get her list, and follow it. It's as simple as that."

Right. His grandmother was going into the home and wouldn't be coming back out. It was as simple as that.

"Delegate the things you can't do yourself."

"To who, Mom? Mandy's at Duke. What can she do?"

"Carl," his father cut in, "I know this wasn't what you were expecting, but don't take it out on your mother."

An Asian man wearing a clerical collar approached the building and smiled. Carl nodded and moved to the side to murmur the expected apology to his mother.

"You can use the family credit card to hire movers and pay for whatever repairs need to be done to the house. What-ever you think is necessary."

After a few more instructions from his parents, Carl disconnected and shoved the phone into his pocket. Life had just gotten incredibly more complicated. His fingers brushed against stiff cardboard, and he pulled out the business card the director had given him. Fine. He had someone to help him. Since his parents were paying for it, he hoped the company was expensive.

"Excuse me," a voice came from behind him. The man in the clerical collar stepped forward. "I don't want to intrude, but are you Jean Northam's grandson? I'm Andy Tran from Keeney United Methodist Church, and she's one of my parishioners. Is she alright?" Then he looked closely at Carl. "Are you alright?"

"Fine," Carl replied and forced a smile.

Andy leaned closer. "Truly fine? Or Fucked-up, Insecure, Neurotic, and Emotional fine?"

Carl sputtered. "Are you really a pastor?"

"Yeah, they'll let anybody in these days. Seriously, though, can I help with anything?"

The man looked so sincere, Carl allowed himself to be guided to a bench facing a small pond. They sat and watched the ducks, Andy not saying anything while Carl collected his thoughts.

"Gram is going into assisted living instead of coming home," he said.

"Is the congestive heart failure worsening?"

Carl looked at Andy. "You knew?"

"You didn't?"

Carl's shoulders sagged, and he shook his head. "No. My parents just told me."

Andy nodded, crossing one leg over the other and settling back against the bench. "Miss Jean told me shortly after she got the diagnosis some months ago."

"Why didn't anyone tell me?" He tried to keep the whine out of his voice but wasn't sure how successful he was. "I would have…"

"What? What would you have done? Made it better? Made it go away?"

Carl flashed him an irritated glance. "No, but I would have visited more often. Maybe helped her with… something."

"Your grandmother is one of the most independent women I know. If she needed help, she would have asked for it."

"Maybe."

"And now that she does need help, you're here."

"Yeah," Carl grunted and scowled at a duck that waddled toward them looking for food. "I just…feel like I've been blindsided, like telling *me* that Gram was sick wasn't a high priority."

"Maybe. Or maybe there was a reason you weren't told sooner. Maybe Miss Jean didn't want you to know."

Carl turned his scowl on the pastor. "Why wouldn't she?" The guy really sucked at the tea and sympathy thing. Had he skipped that class in seminary school?

"There's not much to be done for congestive heart failure. Maybe she wanted to protect you from bad news for as long as possible."

His scowl turned into a frown as he considered Andy's words, and he nodded slowly. "Yeah, maybe."

They watched the ducks in silence for a few moments, and then Andy rose and clapped him on the shoulder. "If you want to talk, you can usually find me at the coffee shop on Main Street most afternoons."

"Not at the church?"

"The church office was being renovated, so I started taking my laptop to the coffee shop. One day, I was coming from a meeting with the conference and had this on." He pointed to his clerical collar. "It's quite the conversation starter. People ask if it's real and why I want to be a pastor, especially when they find out I'm gay. A lot of people don't have good experiences with the church and want to process those experiences with someone. So I listen and maybe pray with them, if they ask. I wouldn't have those opportunities if I stayed in my office. Also, the wifi is better than at the church." He grinned, handed Carl a business card, and headed off.

Carl turned the card over in his hand, feeling slightly better for the conversation. Then he pulled out his phone to look up congestive heart failure.

He returned to Gram's room to find a woman with dark hair and a curvy figure leading his grandmother through some exercises. He caught a flash of golden skin. "Sylvie?"

The woman turned and smiled. Not Sylvie, but someone

obviously closely related to her. "Nope," she said. "I'm Cara. Sylvie's my sister."

Now that she said that, he noticed the differences. Cara was taller, had her hair in a no-nonsense braid, wore a single, small gold hoop instead of a parade of studs going up each ear, and gave off a much more relaxed vibe.

Grinning from ear to ear, Gram said, "This is my grandson Carl, and he's single."

"Gram!" Carl rolled his eyes and mouthed "Sorry" to Cara.

She winked in return, looking amused. "Thanks, Miss Jean, but I have a girlfriend."

"Oh." Not to be deterred, Gram said, "How serious is it? Because my granddaughter is a lesbian and she's studying for her PhD. But I don't know. Carl, is Mandy seeing anyone right now?"

"Gram!"

"What? Cara is wonderful. She's a physiotherapist, owns her own home, and would make a wonderful granddaughter-in-law."

She also had a sense of humor. Helping Gram to sit up, she said, "Sierra and I are pretty serious, but if it doesn't work out, you can show me pictures of your granddaughter. How does that sound?"

"Deal," Gram said.

Cara winked at Carl again before leaving him alone with his grandmother.

Gram pointed at a lined tablet on the bedside table and said, "Hand that to me, please. I take it you were talking to Debra?"

He did as told and sat in the folding chair next to her hospital bed. "Yeah."

She flipped through the pages on the notepad, and he saw the many details of her to-do list. "I knew this day would be coming, so I started thinking about where I'd like to be.

There are four facilities in Keeney that are popular, so I toured them about a year ago with some ladies from church. We'd make a day trip out of it. If you book an official tour, they offer you lunch. So that's what we did. Then we'd go home, take a nap, and meet for supper to compare notes."

"That's…that's very thorough."

"Um-hmm. It helps that I knew a lot of the residents and staff and could get the real skinny from them." She flipped through the sheets again, then ripped a page out and handed it to Carl. "This is what I want from the house. This—" she handed him another sheet "—is the list of who you need to contact."

In addition to a moving company, a realtor, Gram's financial advisor, and her pastor, there were her bridge partners and the neighbor who cut her lawn. Very thorough indeed. But it didn't make it feel any better.

"Sweetheart," Gram said, her tone less business-like, "I'm not dying tomorrow, so no need to look so mournful."

"Gram—"

"I know, I know." She patted his hand. "You came to Keeney thinking you were just going to help me at home while I recovered. You are helping me, it's just going to be in a different place, and it might take a little longer."

Blinking back tears, he stared at her work-worn hands. The hands that had prepared endless meals for him and knit industriously while she supervised his homework looked tiny compared to his. But they were still strong and still supporting him. He turned his palm over and squeezed her hand gently. "Okay. Walk me through your list."

CHAPTER 6

Sylvie hurried out of her office door and Kegeled her way to the bathroom, knowing that if she put it off any longer, she'd risk a UTI. Relief allowed her to move a bit more slowly on the return trip, and the male voices from the break room drew her attention.

Her brother's rough growl was easy to identify. Tomas always sounded like he was pissed off at the world, or maybe it was just when he spoke with anyone other than Fiona. He had smiles aplenty for his wife. It still boggled her mind to think that her badass brother, who'd barely made it through high school, now taught home repair classes to senior citizens and was married to a woman with an MBA.

She knew part of it had to do with Vincent. The two had met in prison and formed a fast friendship that had only strengthened when they both started working at KBS. The combination of First Nations and Latino blood made Vincent Ortiz devastatingly handsome, and Sylvie had crushed on him when she was younger. But he'd fallen hard for Hilary, and it was hard to say who smiled brighter when the two were together.

Right now, Vincent sounded amused at whatever was

annoying Tomas, laughter bubbling between his indistinct words.

"Ouch!"

Was that Carl?

She poked her head into the room, wondering what they were up to and hoping it wasn't anything that required her help. Sleep was not her friend these days, and it was hard enough to get her own work done without an abundance of caffeine. Hence, a need for a bathroom break.

"You'll get a better grip if you use the sides, not the tip," Vincent said.

"Ouch," Carl said again. "Quit pinching me."

"Then stop squirming," Tomas replied.

"What are you doing?" Sylvie asked, coming into the room to stand at the end of the table for a better look. Carl faced the wall of windows overlooking the store, his shirt yanked up and his pants sagging open to reveal one firm butt cheek. Tomas sat in a chair, inspecting said butt cheek, while Vincent stood to the side, alternately giggling and providing direction.

All three heads turned her way. Vincent smiled, Tomas frowned, and Carl looked like he wanted to crawl into a hole. Confronted with an expanse of gleaming dark skin over firm muscles, it was hard to look away, but Sylvie managed, raising her gaze to fix on Vincent's grin.

"The kid got a splinter in his ass and Tomas is pulling it out," Vincent said.

"More like torturing me," Carl complained.

Fighting to hold back her own grin, Sylvie asked, "How did you—and are you using pliers?" She shook her head with disgust as she retrieved the first aid kit from a cupboard above the counter that held the coffee machine. Opening the kit on the table, she found tweezers and alcohol wipes and held them out to her brother. "Use the right tools. I can just see the insurance report if he gets an infection. How'd you do it anyway?"

Vincent snickered and spots of red burnished Carl's cheeks. "I'll tell you some other time," he muttered.

Tomas's gaze moved from the small tweezers to Carl's ass before he looked up at Sylvie. "This is not in my job description, so I'll hold the light and you do it."

"Me?" Sylvie's voice rose an octave as Tomas vacated the chair and pushed her into it. She was now inches away from more of Carl than she'd ever thought she'd see. A flush rose up her neck, and she was sure her face was as red as his.

His Adam's apple bobbed as he looked down at her with wide eyes. That hint of nervous embarrassment on his part was enough to alleviate her own.

Pulling on a pair of disposable gloves, she opened an alcohol wipe. "This might sting a bit," she said.

"It's fine," he replied, but flinched when she put a hand on his hip and smoothed the wipe across the inflamed area. Goosebumps rose, and tiny hairs stood erect on his otherwise smooth skin, and he shivered. She was tempted to blow on it to see how he'd react.

A light came on, and Tomas's voice broke through the lascivious thought. "I count three slivers," he said.

Sylvie swallowed and nodded. "Yep. I do too." She picked up the tweezers, and her eyes met Carl's. "Sorry. This is probably going to hurt."

"It's fine." He sighed. "Let's just get this over with."

Thank God for the presence of Tomas and Vincent. Tomas held the light steady and passed gauze pads to her when blood oozed in the wake of one stubborn, tiny piece of wood. Vincent kept up a constant chatter, distracting Carl with tales of all his injuries from skateboarding, showing off some of his more impressive scars as Sylvie poked and pulled.

Finally, it was done, and she smoothed Band-Aids over

the extractions, tempted to plant a kiss over the injured area, but settled for patting Carl's hip.

Vincent and Tomas wandered off, and Carl righted his clothing before helping Sylvie tidy up.

"Thank you," he said, rubbing absently at his injured behind. "I owe you."

"Oh, you definitely do," she agreed. It was much easier to speak when he was dressed. However, she'd seen the dimples on either side of his spine and knew the satiny feel of his skin, and that knowledge wouldn't go away. "And I think you can start by telling me how you got them."

*H*ands on his hips, he stared at the floor, then squinted up at her. "Promise not to laugh?"

"No. I don't make promises I know I can't keep." Her smirk was the first smile he'd seen on her in days.

The Sylvie he remembered was bouncy, energetic, and enthusiastic. Since his return, he had yet to see that side of her. Considering the crap she'd been going through, providing a laugh at his expense wasn't a bad thing.

"So, you know I'm staying at my grandmother's house. It was hot last night, and I was sitting out on the back deck having a beer. When I took the cap off, it rolled off to the side, out of my reach. So I scooted over to get it—" he shifted his hips to one side, mimicking the action "—then scooted back—" he shifted to the other side "—and that's when the deck bit me in the ass."

Sylvie frowned at him. "They went right through your pants? What were you wearing?"

Carl looked away, rubbing his hand over his jaw. "Nothing," he murmured.

Sylvie cupped one ear. "I'm sorry, I don't think I heard you correctly. You were naked?"

"Yeah. It was a nice night, and all my clothes were in the washer or the dryer. Besides, it was dark. No one could see me."

Clearly fighting a smile, she stared at him.

"At least, I don't think so."

"Okay," she said, eyes sparkling. "I won't laugh. At least not in front of you."

He followed her to the door, where she stopped and looked back over her shoulder.

"Just umm, maybe use a chair next time." She twitched her hips from side to side and sashayed out, trailing giggles behind her.

Carl was a little fuzzy on the number, but more than one beer led up to the splinter situation. He wasn't fuzzy on why he'd been drinking in the dark, though.

His mother had bombarded him with emails all damn day, wanting status updates on Gram and questioning his decisions about the house. Between those headache-inducing demands were messages from Dean suggesting they get together. Those were harder to respond to than his mother's emails because, after learning more about the crown prince of Sanchez Homes, he wanted to say, *Hell to the power of No!* However, that reply would tank his career with Build Clean.

Getting Gram settled was a convenient excuse, but he needed to come up with something better. In truth, what he really needed was to be taken out of the loop between Sanchez Homes and Build Clean. He wouldn't be in Keeney too much longer, so he just needed to find a way to keep his head down while navigating the small town drama of Sylvie and Dean without getting involved or damaging his career.

He washed his hands in the bathroom and propped a hip against the sink. Immediately, he jerked back from the contact, rubbing a hand against the injured area. He'd intended to visit an urgent care in another town where he could remain anonymous. But those nosey nellies, Vincent and Tomas, noticed right away that he was moving gingerly and wouldn't leave him alone until he'd told them. Then they'd practically peed themselves laughing. It was times like these that he missed Olympia, where he could get lost in the crowds and nurse his humiliation in private. Instead, he'd bared his ass in front of coworkers.

Worse than being the butt of their jokes (ha ha) was Sylvie touching him. While trying to be efficient, she'd been tender and caring. A side of her he'd never seen before. At one point, she'd bent so close, her breath tickled his skin, making him shiver. The sensation was almost too much, and he'd welcomed the pain of her removing the splinters because it was all that kept him from springing a boner. Sylvie probably didn't realize the effect she had on him. And he resolved to keep it that way. He did not need another complication.

CHAPTER 7

Sylvie answered the ringing phone. "Yo, bitch. Where are you? If you're not here in five minutes, I'm starting on the wine without you."

"Sylvie?"

She bolted up from the couch, nearly dropping her phone. "Hi, Mom."

"That is not the way to answer the phone."

"Sorry! I thought it was Cara."

"And you call your sister 'bitch?'"

Listening as her mother chastised her in a torrent of Spanish, she shuffled over to the kitchen and banged her head against the counter. A tap at the door drew her eye. *Thank God.* Cara held a bag of takeout in one hand and a box of Okanagan Porchbanger in the other. Good, because she didn't think a single bottle of cheap wine would be enough for the evening.

Sylvie opened the door while putting the phone on speaker so that Cara could enjoy their mother's tirade. Her sister rolled her eyes in sympathy, put the food and wine on the counter, and started opening cupboards.

A few years older than Sylvie, Cara was focused, hardworking, and seemed to have had her ducks in a row since preschool. In their mother's eyes, Cara could do no wrong. She found plates, wineglasses, cutlery, and napkins and proceeded to set the table.

Done venting about Sylvie's atrocious language and phone manners, Louisa Santiago switched to a different topic. "What's this about you throwing a tantrum downtown the other day?"

Sylvie cringed. Her parents might be a thousand miles away and in another time zone, but her mother rarely missed anything. Wide-eyed, Cara handed her a wineglass filled to the brim. "Sounds like you need this," she murmured.

"I didn't have a tantrum, Mom," Sylvie said into the phone while smiling her thanks at Cara. "Dean and I had a…heated discussion."

Her mother's voice was steely. "You kicked in his car door, Sylvie. That's more than a discussion."

In the background, her dad said, "The Tesla? No great loss."

"It wasn't the Tesla," Sylvie replied. "It wasn't the Tesla," she said again, more quietly. Realization struck her. *Shit!* She hadn't kicked in Dean's car.

"Not the Tesla?" Her father had grabbed the phone. "What was it then?" Carlos Santiago had been rebuilding and reselling cars for years and now owned an automotive supply store. He had a passion for anything built before the advent of computer technology and a particular disdain for electric vehicles.

"It was an Audi," she replied. "I think it was his dad's."

Sylvie gulped her wine as her parents digested the information, and Cara put her arm around her shoulder in solidarity.

"What were you thinking?" their mother shouted. "You need to apologize and pay for the repairs."

"Tell Ron to bring it by the shop. I'll have one of the guys take care of it," her dad added.

"Wait," Cara jumped in. "Don't you want to hear Sylvie's side? I'm sure she's got a good reason."

"Cara? You're there too? How are you? How's Sierra? Have you set a date?"

Grateful for the brief reprieve, Sylvie considered how much of her situation to reveal to her parents.

She and Cara winning the 50/50 was a godsend. Cara had sensibly used her money to purchase a townhouse. Sylvie planned to use her money to finance her dream. While working as Hilary Ortiz's administrative assistant at KBS was a good job, and she truly liked the people she worked with, she wanted to be her own boss.

Flipping houses was risky, which was why she'd continue mudding and taping. It wasn't easy money, and her side hustle had been a bone of contention with Dean. She worked late hours and would return home dirty, her arms and shoulders aching, too exhausted to do more than have a hasty shower and crawl into bed. However, she'd built up a reputation for quality work and had a list of satisfied clients. And for once, her parents held her up as an example, rather than fret about her checkered work history.

After telling their parents that she was fine, Sierra was fine, and that they hadn't set a date for the wedding, Cara glanced meaningfully at Sylvie.

There was no point in not telling them about Dean because if her mom didn't hear about it from someone else, she'd learn about it from Marcia and Iris, two of her good friends. But telling her parents that Dean weaseled her out of her savings because she'd been a moron and hadn't bothered to read the paper she was signing, would worry them to the point they'd cut short their vacation.

"I caught Dean cheating on me and I kicked him out." Into the silence that greeted her bald statement, she added, "then he pissed off the building superintendent and got me evicted from my apartment."

"That asshole," Cara muttered.

"Right?!?" Sylvie muttered back.

Neither of her parents was quick-tempered, but they had long memories. Dean Sanchez would no longer receive free meals at her mother's restaurant or discounts on auto supplies.

"Are you okay, sweetheart? Where are you now? At home?"

Her mother's concern nearly set Sylvie off on a crying jag. She bit a trembling lip and confessed, "It's been a lot. Iris offered her suite, so I'll be fine. Then she and Marcia moved me—honestly, I don't know how I'll be able to pay them back."

"And I'm here," Cara added. "I brought food and wine, and she can sob all over me about that asswipe." Sylvie swatted her. "What? I never did like Dean. He's too smarmy."

Their dad said, "You tell Iris and Marcia their next tune-up is on me."

"Thanks, Dad."

"Sweetheart?" their mother asked, "Do you need any money?"

Sylvie choked back a laugh. If they only knew. Hopefully, though, she'd have it sorted and the money back in her account before they returned from vacation. "No, Mom," she said.

They said their goodbyes, and Sylvie disconnected, relieved to have gotten that over with. She reached for her wine, but Cara grabbed it and held it away from her.

"Hey!"

"Uh-uh. You're lying. No wine until you tell me everything."

"You're evil."

"I am," Cara agreed. "Now spill."

Growing up, their mother had always told them that sharing a burden lightened the load. Sylvie believed the adage and was happy to listen to others and help where she could, but as she got older, she shied away from revealing her own troubles, believing that grown-ass women should be able to sort themselves out.

Cara sipped from her wineglass and then from Sylvie's, as if making a point.

"Fine. I'll—"

The door opened after a cursory knock, revealing Iris and Marcia.

"You're supposed to wait to be invited in," Iris scolded.

"I'm saving time," Marcia replied. "Besides, I brought wine." She hefted a bottle and smiled. "How ya doing, sweetheart? I hear things have been a bit rough."

Iris dropped a plate of cookies on the counter and patted Sylvie's hand. "We thought you might need the company." Then she smiled at Cara. "Well, more company."

In looks and disposition, the two women were polar opposites. Always dressed in bold, bright colors, Marcia vibrated with energy. Iris tended toward baggy mom jeans, orthopedic sneakers, pale colors, and cardigans that seemed to have a never-ending supply of fresh tissues in the pockets. She was tentative to Marcia's decisiveness, but was thoughtful, kind, and generous.

They'd shared many heartaches over the span of their long friendship, but also had running jokes that were older than Sylvie. Many times, she'd come into the store to find one or the other snorting with laughter, leaning on the customer service counter for support. Ali would roll his eyes and shake his head, but he was unable to keep the smile off his own face. "Listening to you two," he'd say, "who would believe that you're respected community members? No one. That's who." His words would only make them laugh harder. And while she had no idea what they were talking about, their giggle fest always made Sylvie smile.

Cara got down two more wineglasses. "Your timing is perfect. Sylvie was just about to tell me what happened."

Three expectant faces turned Sylvie's way. "What do you know?" she asked.

"Ali told me he saw you and Dean having a heated discussion outside the bank the other day," Marcia said.

"Heated? She kicked in his car door," Cara added, snorting.

Sylvie cringed. Her new landlady and boss did not need to know that.

"I'm sure he deserved it," Marcia said staunchly. "I don't think Ali saw that. Carl might have, though."

Wonderful. *Carl* had witnessed her meltdown. If she hadn't plucked splinters out of his butt that day, she'd be more embarrassed. It seemed they were making a habit of seeing each other at their worst.

"You've told me about Ali," Cara said. "But who's Carl? And why are you making that face?"

"I'm not making a face!" Sylvie protested, pressing her fingers against her eyebrows to force them back into their natural position.

Marcia and Iris told her sister about Carl's history and why he was back in Keeney.

"Who's his grandmother?" Cara asked.

"Jean Northam," Iris answered.

Sylvie started opening the bag of takeout. Knowing Cara, there was more than enough food to feed the unexpected guests. She gestured for the others to join her, and they all took seats at the table.

"A young guy came to see Miss Jean while I was with her," Cara said, helping herself to some pad Thai. "He looked like Donald Glover's younger brother. Would that be Carl?"

"Who's Donald Glover?" Iris asked.

Marcia whipped out her phone, found an image of the handsome actor, and turned it to Iris, who nodded slowly. The three began a discussion of Donald Glover's acting career while Sylvie thought about Carl. He was a genuinely nice guy, while she was a mess. Had he seen her kick in the car? He hadn't let on today, and it certainly didn't seem like he'd told Tomas about it. Her brother would have grilled her seven ways to Sunday.

"Ali told me that you and Dean were arguing about money," Marcia said, holding up a hand. "And before you accuse Ali of being an old busybody, he wasn't gossiping. He's just concerned about you."

She needed to tell Iris, and was intending to tell Cara, so why not Marcia as well? Swallowing her food, she sat back and told them about her discovery in the bank. She finished with, "Iris, if you can wait a few days, I can pay the rent on Friday."

"That's fine, dear," Iris said. "I'm just so sorry you're going through this."

Sylvie thanked her with a watery smile. If anyone knew about being betrayed by someone close, it was Iris. Her only child, Eddie, was in jail for embezzling from KBS.

"Will you be able to get your money back?" Cara asked.

"Yes. Andrea, the bank manager, called this afternoon and said that the blonde bimbo was fired, but did confess to never having witnessed me sign the document. So, I will get my money back, but Andrea couldn't give me an exact date. And that means I can't make an offer on that duplex I want to flip."

The women made sympathetic noises but wisely didn't try to jolly Sylvie out of her funk. She listened with half an ear while they talked about people they had in common, and the conversation eventually came back around to Jean Northam, who would be moving into assisted living rather than returning to her own house.

"Jean is incredibly organized and gave Carl a detailed to-do list, but I'm worried he's going to be overwhelmed. He has to pack up the stuff that she wants for her new place, get rid of what's left behind, then prepare the house for sale," Iris said.

Marcia topped off the wineglasses before saying, "I don't see what the problem is, Carl's got a good head on his shoulder. He can handle it."

"Yes, he does, but this is his grandmother's house, and it's full of memories. It may not be easy for him to just pack them up and get rid of them. And Jean has been in that house for almost fifty years. Who knows how much work needs to be done before they can sell it?" Iris replied.

"He's got family. Can't they help?" Sylvie remembered him telling her about a sister.

Iris shook her head. "His parents are overseas, and Mandy is in North Carolina. It's just Carl and he's got a big job waiting for him, so he can't take his time."

"Let me check my calendar," Marcia said, picking up her phone. "I can certainly organize a crew to move Jean into her new place, but I can't commit to helping Carl pack. You and I have that trip to Vancouver to see Michael Buble."

"Right," Iris said. "Let me check with—"

"There's someone in this room who owes you two a huge favor," Cara said, pointing her wineglass at Sylvie and looking at her with wide-eyed innocence. "I bet *she* can help out."

Sylvie narrowed her eyes at her sister before turning a smile on Iris and Marcia. "Sure. I'd be happy to."

CHAPTER 8

The following Saturday, Carl stared at the contents of the dresser drawer. "Oh, hell to the power of no." He was not going to touch his grandmother's underwear. Nope. No way. No how. He'd let Marcia's friend Sybil take care of that.

He couldn't be more ecstatic that Marcia was sending someone to assist him. Packing up the kitchenware was easy. Linens—piece of cake. Clothing? Not so much. Gram was a stylish woman, and particular. She would not be wearing sweatpants and baggy shirts just because she was in assisted living.

The doorbell rang, and he uttered a prayer of thanksgiving as he made his way to answer it. A smile fixed in place, he swung the door open. "Hi, I'm Carl. You must be…Sybil?"

Sylvie Santiago cocked a brow and looked behind her. "Is someone else joining us?"

He held up a finger and pulled out his phone. "Hang on. Let me check with Marcia." Heat climbed up his neck as he shot off a text. And waited. And waited.

"Do you want me to wait out here or shall I get started?"

"Sorry! Marcia said Sybil would be here, and I thought it

was one of her church lady friends…not *you*." She gave him a withering look. "Not that I'm not happy for your help, it's just…"

While he blathered away like an idiot, Sylvie pressed a few keys then put her phone to her ear. "Hi, Marcia. Carl was expecting someone named Sybil, not me."

She listened, then said, "That's what I thought. Thanks. Talk to you later." She disconnected, saying. "Autocorrect hijacked her phone. You're stuck with me."

His ears were so hot, he thought they'd catch fire. Standing aside to allow her to enter, the end of Sylvie's ponytail tickled his upper arm as she brushed past, like it was laughing at him.

Sylvie stood in the middle of the living room and looked around. Carl had been staying there since he'd arrived in Keeney and had left a clutter of personal items on the usually pristine coffee table and a hoodie hanging over the back of the couch. For the first time, he noticed the plants he'd failed to water and the dust collecting on the mantel. Hopefully, Sylvie didn't.

She walked to the kitchen, plopped her tote bag on the counter, and sorted through it before pulling out two packs of stickers: one green, the other red. She said, "Unless you have another plan, I thought you could put green stickers on the stuff you're taking to your grandmother, and red stickers on the stuff that will be donated."

"That's an excellent idea. Thanks."

Sylvie's lips tipped up in a small smile. "It *is* a great idea, but I can't take credit for it. I saw it on one of those decluttering videos." She handed over the stickers. "What can I do while you do that?"

The flush that had subsided rose up his cheeks again. He gestured, and Sylvie followed him into the bedroom. "That," he said, pointing at the open dresser drawer.

She plucked up a pair of neatly folded underwear and let

them unfurl like a white flag of surrender. "Can't deal with granny panties, huh?"

He shook his head vehemently, and her laughter rang out. "For a guy who likes to wander around naked, I wouldn't think it was a problem. How is your owie, anyway?"

While Vincent had razzed him about it for a few days and then let it go, every time Carl stripped down and saw the bandages, the memory of Sylvie touching him returned. "All healed."

"Glad to hear it." Her eyes crinkled, and she gestured at the dresser. "I can take care of this. Did your grandmother give you a list of specific clothing items?"

"Yeah." Carl pulled the list out of his pocket and handed it over. An awareness crept up his arm as their fingers touched briefly. If Sylvie noticed, she gave no indication.

He left her alone to deal with Gram's clothing, feeling better already.

Armed with a package of stickers and Gram's list of things to keep, he set to work in the living room, poking through cupboards and shelves he hadn't looked at in years. She wasn't a hoarder, but Gram certainly kept some interesting things. He found folders containing high school projects and report cards for Mandy and him, half-finished needlework projects, and numerous old wall calendars.

One ear listening for Sylvie, he perched on the coffee table and leafed through a calendar from ten years ago. About the time he and Mandy had come to live with Gram. For every month, each of the squares was filled with Gram's small, neat handwriting. Listed in bullet points were Mandy's piano recitals, his ball games, Gram's church activities, and other things that were important to his grandmother at the time.

One entry made him snort: *Carl to emergency.* He'd slammed his thumb in a car door, and blood had pooled beneath his throbbing thumbnail. Gram took him to the emergency room, where the nurse—of course—was a friend of hers. They'd carried on a conversation while the nurse drilled his thumbnail with a heated paperclip. Carl didn't remember, but had been told that he'd turned white as a sheet during the process.

The calendars were not on the list of things Gram wanted to keep, but instead of slapping a red sticker on them, Carl set them on the couch, deciding to go through the memory keepers later that evening.

A while later, Sylvie wheeled a suitcase into the living room. "Done," she said, looking around the room. "How'd you do?"

Sorting through Gram's things had brought up many memories, and he'd wondered if that had been deliberate on her part. His teenage years were laid out in photographs and keepsakes that he examined and touched, and they now lay in a pile on the coffee table.

Sylvie picked up a framed photo of him in his cap and gown, with one arm around Gram and the other around Mandy. "Is this your high school graduation?"

He nodded.

"Your parents weren't there?"

"Nope. I think they were in Dubai."

Sylvie placed the photo back on the pile and picked up a more recent one. It was him, in a hard hat and tool belt, again with his arm around Gram, who also wore a hard hat. "When was this taken?"

He smiled broadly. "She came to a jobsite and insisted on a tour. It was my first day as a lead contractor, and she brought lunch for the crew."

Sylvie pointed at the green stickers on the stack of framed photographs, then gestured around the room. "Just how big is your grandmother's new place?"

About 70 percent of the room's contents had green stickers, including the couch, two recliners, the bulky coffee table, two end tables, two lamps, and a curio cabinet filled with china teacups. "It was all on her list." His sense of accomplishment dissipated as he imagined moving furniture and boxes into the new place only to have to move them back out because they didn't fit. "Crap," he said.

"Instead of taking *all* the knick-knacks and framed pictures, you could photograph them and create a photo album for her," Sylvie suggested. "That way she could look at them whenever she wants, without the stuff taking up space."

It was a good idea, but it also meant more work. Resentment that his mother had left him in this position coursed through him, to be quickly replaced by guilt. Because half the photos were pictures of him. Considering Gram had practically raised him during his teenage years, the time it would take to get her settled was not a sacrifice. He sighed and nodded.

Sylvie patted his arm, then picked up her bag. "Nothing needs to be decided at the moment. Come on. Let's get something to eat."

His stomach growling in agreement, Carl followed her out to her car. She didn't ask for his opinion, nor tell him where they were going. And it was nice. Nice not to have to make a decision. Nice to roll down the windows and ride in a car on a nice day with a pretty girl who smelled like sunshine. He closed his eyes and inhaled, simply enjoying the moment.

A hand squeezing his knee woke him. Blinking against the sunlight, he glanced around to see Sylvie grinning at him. "Oh, hey. Did I snore?"

"No," she answered, "but you might want to wipe that drool off your chin."

His hand came away dry when he swiped at his face. "Ha ha."

Climbing out of the car, he stretched and looked up at the building in front of him. A sign written in big, bold letters announced, Hola!

"It's my mom's restaurant," Sylvie said. "Have you ever been here?"

"Yes, but it was years ago."

Inside the restaurant, Sylvie greeted the hostess by name, and they were led to a booth by the window. The place was hopping with a mixed crowd of retirees and businesspeople, all tucking into mouth-watering Mexican food.

A short, barrel-shaped woman emerged from the kitchen dressed in a stained chef's coat and beelined toward them. She scooted Sylvie over on the bench seat to sit beside her. "What's this about you kicking the shit out of Dean Sanchez on Main Street?" she demanded in Spanish.

Carl choked back a laugh and stared at his menu. He'd learned Spanish while working construction alongside Tomas—starting with the curse words.

Sylvie shushed her, replying, "I didn't kick the shit out of Dean, and I don't want to talk about it. Not in front of him. He's a coworker."

"Yeah? I thought maybe you'd moved on to greener pastures. And I wouldn't blame you. He's a tall drink of water, a little young maybe, but very cute. Is he even legal yet?"

Carl put the menu down and said in Spanish, "I'm twenty-four."

The woman appeared to be in her late forties. She looked him over, grinned, and extended a hand. "I'm Stevie."

"Carl," he said, shaking her hand. "She kicked Dean's car, not him."

Sylvie held the menu up so high that all he could see was the top of her head.

"Too bad, the asshat deserves to be taken down a peg or two," Stevie murmured. Someone called her name from the kitchen, and she rose from the table. She gave Sylvie's shoulder a slight shake and said, "You're well rid of him. Now don't be a stranger."

To Carl, she said, "I'll send over the special. On the house," and gave him a look that he took to mean, *if you hurt her, I will come after you with a meat cleaver.*

He swallowed, nodded, and watched her leave.

A server brought them chips, salsa, and glasses of water, asked if they wanted anything else, then departed.

Sylvie gulped down her water and then toyed with her cutlery. "Sorry about that," she said. "Stevie can be a bit much."

"No worries." He almost wished they'd gone somewhere else. Somewhere Sylvie wouldn't be reminded of the crap she was going through. Wanting a return to the easy camaraderie they'd had earlier, he lounged against the back of the booth and gave her his cockiest smile. "I was tempted to let you think I couldn't understand you and hear what else you had to say about me."

"Why would we talk about you?"

"Well, I am very cute."

A wadded-up napkin hit him square in the chest. "To older women, maybe." Her smile took the sting out of her words.

He stroked his chin like he was considering her words. "They are my demographic. Now, how to capitalize on that...?"

His levity had the desired effect, and he was pleased she looked more relaxed. Their meal arrived, and they ate mostly in companionable silence. He mentioned the dusty drywall equipment in the back of her Subaru, and she told him about her side hustle. Her drive and work ethic were impressive. Most people he knew were content to hold down one job.

They finished their meals and went into the kitchen, where Sylvie was greeted with warm hugs. Stevie and another cook grilled her more about Dean, her plans, and whether she needed help. Sylvie patiently answered all their questions without getting annoyed, and they left after another round of hugs.

"Doesn't it bother you?" Carl asked as they got into the car. "The way they're all up in your business?"

"Sometimes. But they're family, and I know they care about me. If I asked, they'd drop everything to help me out. However," she rolled her eyes dramatically, "there would be a lot of opinions on how I should do things. So I don't ask."

She backed out of the parking space and asked, "What's the name of your grandmother's new place?"

"Cascades Lodge. Why?"

"Wanna stop by and scope out the joint? See how big her apartment will be, and maybe take measurements? That way we'll know what pieces of furniture will fit and how much wall space is available for photographs."

"Good idea, let's do it." What was even better was her use of "we." She was jumping in to help without being asked. Was she even aware that she'd done so?

The assisted living portion of Cascades Lodge buzzed with energetic octogenarians. Sylvie had dodged more walkers and scooters in ten minutes than she had in her entire lifetime. Carl was not the first family member to face the problem of where to put all their loved ones' belongings, and the facility had two model suites reserved for display purposes. One was a studio, and the other was a one-bedroom apartment.

The doorways were wide, the low-pile carpeting was limited to the bedroom, and handrails were installed in the spacious bathroom. Sylvie had no idea what the rent was for a place like this, but imagined it wasn't cheap.

She was on all fours and holding the end of a measuring tape when someone said, "Knock, knock." Peering over her shoulder, she spotted an elegant redhead entering the suite. The woman was tall and slim, wearing a pristine cream pantsuit, making Sylvie aware that her ample ass was on display. Knowing she'd be helping Carl muck about in his grandmother's house, she'd donned jeans and a T-shirt that had seen better days. Now, she regretted that practical decision. She twisted and sat back on her haunches, crossing her arms to hide a paint stain on her shirt.

"Hi, I'm Kelsey." The woman glanced at Sylvie and flashed a large smile at Carl. "The front desk told me you were here, so I decided to pop in instead of returning your call. I've only got a minute, but would you like to set up a meeting to discuss how we can assist with your grandmother's transition? If it works for you, I'm available at four-thirty today."

"I'll just bet you are," Sylvie mumbled.

Carl asked, "What was that?"

"Nothing. Just, umm, admiring the baseboards."

Two pairs of eyes stared at her like she was an idiot. And she felt like one. Kelsey hadn't said or done anything unprofessional; her presence simply felt like a pinprick bursting a bubble.

The day had turned out better than Sylvie had anticipated. Carl had seemed so out of his depth and then so grateful that focusing on his problems had helped her not focus on her own.

She'd scrutinized her bank statements and credit card accounts to ensure Dean hadn't done more damage. As much as she'd like to believe Andrea that the money would be returned, until she saw it, she was going to worry. She didn't have any mudding jobs lined up either. Something else to spiral about. So packing up Miss Jean's stuff with Carl was a nice distraction.

They'd worked together well, and she'd seen flashes of the

goofy, eager kid she'd worked with years ago. The kid who'd occasionally trip over his tongue while talking to her. It wasn't quite flirting, but an awareness and a gravitation toward each other. Sitting across from him in the restaurant, she'd eyed him surreptitiously. Long and lean, his biceps were nicely formed rather than bulging, and she knew first-hand that his butt was firm. She'd also glimpsed the cutest little belly button the day she removed the splinters.

Carl's attention today was a balm to her wounded pride. If he'd noticed the hostess and server making eyes at him, he hadn't let on. After finding Dean with the blonde, Sylvie had spent too much time wondering if he'd ever cared for her at all, or if she was simply a means to an end.

The woman talking to Carl shifted her stance, revealing red-soled pumps, the kind that cost more than Sylvie's first car. Sylvie shifted her own position, sitting on the floor and stretching out her legs to examine her scuffed and stained Chucks. They'd always looked so incongruous, sitting beside Dean's pristine sneakers. He kept those in boxes that were labeled with the days of the week, like the underwear she'd worn when she was a kid. The sneakers were in addition to the loafers, boots, and flip-flops. Dean had more shoes than she did. But he'd paid his fair share of the rent and picked up the bill when they ate out, so she never bothered him about his spending habits.

That led her to think about bills and stopping by the old apartment for her mail. In the months that he'd lived with her, she'd never once seen a bill for Dean. He either paid everything online or his mail went to his office. Did he, in fact, pay all his bills? Is that why he'd stolen from her?

The whir of the tape measure spooling back up drew Sylvie from her brooding.

"That's the last measurement we need. We can measure the furniture and draw up a floor plan when we get back to the house. Actually, Kelsey said there's an app that allows you to do that. You know, move pieces around to see how they fit." Carl's eyes danced as he moved his hands in the air like he was moving objects.

"Sounds like a plan," Sylvie said before checking her phone. She sighed. "We need to make a stop first."

CHAPTER 9

Carl peered at the imposing structure that housed the offices of Sanchez Homes, then looked over at Sylvie. "Why are we here?" he asked.

"You know that car I kicked?"

"Yeah."

"It belongs to Ron Sanchez."

"Oh," Carl replied, then added. "Oh, shit. That's—"

"Yeah," Sylvie sighed so big, the rosary hanging from her rearview mirror danced. "Sometimes my temper gets the better of me. Now it's time to pay the piper. Hopefully, this won't take long."

"Not a problem. I'll just catch a few Zs." He made a production of reclining his seat and putting his head back while secretly watching Sylvie.

She hauled herself out of the car with a heavy sigh and approached the building on dragging feet. It would be comical if it were someone else. An older man exited the front door and stopped when he saw Sylvie's approach.

Carl turned off the car stereo and lowered the windows. He could hear the man's measured tones and Sylvie's more agitated voice, but couldn't understand their words.

The man, whom he assumed was Ron Sanchez, crossed his arms and shook his head slowly while Sylvie alternated between wringing her hands and gesticulating wildly. The man held up a hand to stop her agitated flow of words, said a few things that made Sylvie stare at the ground, patted her on the shoulder, and left.

Whatever Ron Sanchez said must have sucked because everything from Sylvie's shoulders to her ponytail drooped. Part of Carl wanted to wrap her in a big hug, while another part wanted to pretend he hadn't seen anything and let her keep a smidgen of pride.

Seeing her walking back to the vehicle, he closed his eyes and then popped them open at the slam of a car door.

"So, did you rat me out to my father?" Dean Sanchez asked, strolling toward Sylvie like he didn't have a care in the world.

Sylvie straightened her spine and flicked her ponytail over her shoulder. "It was a lovely conversation. We agreed that you have the moral compass of a sewer rat."

Dean stared from Sylvie to the building behind her and then back to Sylvie. "No. I don't think you did that. I think you told him about me screwing the blonde, which he'll understand because—" he raked a dismissive gaze over her "—given a choice, who wouldn't? But the bank account? Nah. Because both our names are on the account *and* both our signatures."

"That money wasn't yours to take!"

"Babe," Dean crossed his arms and shook his head slowly in an unconscious parody of his father, "It was your contribution to our business. Everyone knows we were going to flip houses together. You talked about it ad nauseam. I just expedited the process."

Caustic and condescending, this was a totally different person from the guy Carl had lunch with. Pleased with himself, like he'd won a competition. If he'd taken money from Sylvie in addition to screwing around on her, it was no wonder she'd kicked his car in. Carl was surprised she hadn't kicked him in the balls.

"But I didn't agree to that!"

"We had a verbal agreement."

"No we didn't!"

Dean shrugged. "It's my word against yours. And now it's my money."

She sputtered, "I'll—I'll—I'll take you to court!"

"No, you won't." He gestured to the building behind them. "Sanchez Homes has excellent lawyers. We'll bury you.

"Oh, and if you try to trash-talk me, I have photos of you. The kind that will make your mother so proud of you."

Sylvie gasped and sputtered, "You do not!"

"Maybe not, but AI can make anything look real."

Dean strolled into the building, leaving Sylvie seething on the sidewalk.

She looked fit to be tied, and Carl wondered whether to go to her or stay in the car, pretending he hadn't heard a thing. However, they'd been way too loud, and Sylvie wouldn't believe him.

Sanchez Homes backed onto a slough that ran through Keeney, linking Lake Washington and Lake Sammamish, and a popular running and biking trail lay between the water and the buildings. Carl climbed out of the car and motioned toward the path. "Wanna take a walk?"

Muttering an expletive, she wheeled around and took off.

He trailed behind her as she stomped past the building to crunch along the gravel path. Walkers, joggers, and cyclists passed them, and Carl waited. She'd either tell him or not; he'd leave it up to her. Regardless, he wasn't going to take Dean up on his invitation to play golf at the country club.

It wasn't a new phenomenon, and he knew it happened all the time, but looking at Sylvie, he wondered how smart people lost their heads and their hearts to asshats.

Her steps faltered, and he heard a sniffle and caught Sylvie wiping her eyes. *Ah shit.* He preferred Angry Sylvie to Sad Sylvie. He pulled a handkerchief from his pocket and handed it to her.

She looked at it in bewilderment. "You carry a handkerchief?"

"I have allergies. Kleenex falls apart in the washing machine, and these don't. And they're better for the environment."

"Thanks," she said, wiping her nose.

Side by side, they continued walking, Carl wishing he could do more than give her a handkerchief.

"So, did—"

"He screwed around on me, got me evicted, and drained my bank account. Yes, I will get the money back, but not in time to buy the house I want. Do I have a legal case? Who knows? Am I an idiot? Absolutely. Did I answer your question?" She spoke so quickly that some of the words slurred together.

"I was gonna ask if you wanted ice cream."

"Oh." She blinked. "Oh," she repeated, "um, yeah. That would be nice."

They got cones and sat on a bench facing a field where a group of people were silently going through Tai Chi. It wasn't apparent who was leading; they simply flowed together.

"Remember when your brother taught his first class to seniors?" Carl nudged her arm. "And that old guy kept annoying you?"

Sylvie snorted. "Mr. Gardiner? He was sweet."

"Sweet? I thought you were going to take his head off. You two argued through the whole class."

"I don't remember it that way. He was a bit of a tease and reminded me of my grandfather. Nice old guy." She twisted around to face him. "Why? What made you think of that?"

"It was the first time we met. All your accessories were pink, and you carried a lip gloss in your tool belt."

Her brow furrowed for a moment, and she laughed. "You remember that?"

He remembered thinking he could watch the impudent sway of her ponytail for the rest of his life. He said, "I thought it was brilliant and started stashing Chapstick in mine."

"Really?"

"Yep." He nodded solemnly. "All the construction workers do it these days. I'm quite the influencer."

She shook her head and licked her ice cream. "Silly man."

There wasn't much he could do about the shit that Dean put her through, but if he could make Sylvie Santiago laugh, he'd take it.

The large, iced mocha wouldn't solve her problems, but the combination of caffeine and chocolate gave her the boost to attempt something productive. She'd prefer to be mudding drywall, but her side business was quiet at the moment, so she'd chosen to clean out her office email and go through work orders.

The store was open until nine pm, and the parking lot was half full when she parked and walked through the doors of KBS, waving at the cashiers.

As she threaded her way through the aisles on her way to the office, a woman rose from a crouch in front of a display of toilet plungers and stepped in front of Sylvie.

Sylvie moved to the side to avoid a collision as the woman turned to face her.

"Oops, sorry about—"

"What the hell are you doing here?" Sylvie stared at the

woman. She wore a KBS polo shirt with a nametag that read "Ingrid."

The woman frowned, then her eyes widened as recognition dawned. "You work here?"

"Uhh. *Yeah.*" Sylvie cocked a hip. "And apparently you do too." She whipped her head around, looking for Ali. But it was late, and he'd clocked out hours ago. Tomorrow. Tomorrow she would break off his arm and beat him with the bloody end. How could he do this to her?

Ingrid's shoulders slumped. The glare of the fluorescents did not flatter anyone and was particularly harsh on the blonde. She looked wan and colorless, a far cry from the confident woman who'd strutted into Andrea's office at the bank. "I got fired."

"Good."

Ingrid flinched.

Sylvie smirked as she stalked past her. Schadenfreude carried her up the stairs and into her office to be replaced by guilt when she reached the big windows. Pushing a hank of limp hair out of her eyes and sinking back to the floor to stock shelves, Ingrid looked small and defeated.

"Shit," Sylvie muttered. Retreating from the window, she fired up her computer to lose herself in work. However, questions whirled in her head. What was Ingrid's story? Had she known about Sylvie when she was screwing Dean? God knows the man was smooth. Sylvie had let him into her bed on the second date, and it wasn't long afterward that he'd become a permanent fixture.

And he'd been decent to her, right up until she'd found him with Ingrid. Was accessing her money the sole reason he'd moved in with her? Three hundred thousand was a fortune to Sylvie, but to Dean? The guy who'd take over Sanchez Homes? It was a drop in a bucket. And yes, he was starting his own business; however, there had to be better ways to raise startup money. A means to an end. That's all she was.

She drifted over to the window, seeking out Ingrid. The store would be closing soon, and she would be leaving. Sylvie had about fifteen minutes to talk to her. If Ingrid answered her questions, maybe Sylvie would be able to sleep tonight. She hurried down the stairs and speed-walked toward her.

"Why were you wearing my underwear?"

Ingrid's head whipped around. "What?"

"My underwear. When I walked in on you and Dean, you had my underwear."

Tears welled in Ingrid's eyes, and she dropped her head. "Can it get any worse?" she muttered.

Sylvie did not want to feel bad for her, but the woman crying on the floor did not match the image that lived rent-free in her head. A naked blonde writhing on Dean's lap.

Carl's handkerchief was in Sylvie's pocket. She'd laundered it and intended to return it, but hadn't seen him in a few days. She handed it to Ingrid, who nodded her thanks and blew her nose with a loud honk.

To give her a bit of privacy, Sylvie stepped away and looked down the aisle. Ingrid hadn't just stocked the shelves, she'd arranged the products in an eye-catching fashion. Not an easy feat with toilet plungers.

Ingrid cleared her throat and said, "I don't remember much about seeing you that day. We were celebrating and I'm not much of a drinker, so…"

Sylvie twisted to face her. "What were you celebrating?"

"Our one-month anniversary," Ingrid replied. "Dean gave me the lingerie and asked me to model it for him and then…" her words trailed off, and she looked away.

"Asshole." Sylvie sighed. "You didn't know about me?"

"He told me he lived with his sister."

"In a one-bedroom apartment?"

Ingrid shrugged. "It was the first time I'd been there."

A cashier announced that the store would be closing and asked customers to make their way to the front.

"What time do you clock out?" Sylvie asked.

"Nine o'clock, but I want to finish these first." Ingrid gestured to a box half-full of drain cleaner, next to a stack of flattened cardboard.

"I have to finish something in the office and then…would you, um, like to go somewhere to talk?"

Ingrid eyed Sylvie warily. "Okay, but it has to be in a public place. I heard what you did to that car."

Half an hour later, Sylvie and Ingrid sat at an outdoor table at Denali's. Originally the first school in Keeney, the stately brick building had been renovated into a hotel, and its outbuildings had been converted into restaurants that surrounded a tree-lined patio. Ingrid had pulled a sweater over her KBS shirt, combed her hair, and put on lipstick, but she still looked haggard. She huddled over a chamomile tea while Sylvie nursed a club soda.

A server set down a basket of bread and a crock of butter, winked at Sylvie, and walked off.

Ingrid frowned. "When did you order that?"

"I didn't," Sylvie replied. "My family owns a restaurant. Our server, and the two over by the bar, pick up shifts for banquets every now and then." She buttered a piece of bread and took a bite, nodding her thanks at the server. "Do you want some?"

Ingrid eyed the breadbasket longingly. "I don't eat bread."

"Suit yourself," Sylvie said, going back for another piece. Someone called her name, and she waved at a group of people clustered around a firepit.

"Do you know everyone?"

"No, but I grew up in Keeney." And worked a lot of different jobs around town, but she didn't say that aloud. "I take it you didn't?"

"I'm from Wenatchee. I transferred to Keeney when there

was an opening at the bank for a loans officer. I was only there four months before…"

The bread in Sylvie's mouth lost all its flavor, and she took a drink to wash it down. "Before you got fired."

"Yeah." Ingrid sighed.

Sylvie pushed the bread toward her. "Eat. You look like you're going to blow away." Aside from her breasts, the woman was skin and bones.

"I shouldn't. Dean says he likes me—" Her eyes went big as she looked at Sylvie.

"Go ahead. Finish the sentence. What does *Dean* like?"

"He says he likes his women long and lean," she rushed out.

In the seventh grade, Sylvie was the tallest girl in her class. Then she stopped growing. At five feet nothing, and with thick thighs and a generous behind, no one would describe her as long and lean. "That's funny. He told me he liked a woman with something to hold onto."

They stared at each other silently, laughter rising up behind them from the firepit.

"Which do you think was the truth?" Ingrid asked.

"I think," Sylvie said slowly, "that he'd say whatever would get him what he wanted."

Ingrid looked down and sniffed quietly, wiping at her eyes with the handkerchief.

Carl's handkerchief. Would it be tacky to ask for it back? Probably. Sylvie would buy him a new one. Maybe one for herself, too. They came in handy.

"You really liked him, didn't you?"

Ingrid nodded. "I thought…I thought we…" Her shoulders shook as her words faded away.

Seeing the outpouring of emotion, Sylvie's heart hurt. She hadn't cried over Dean. She'd cried for allowing herself to be used by him, for not seeing past his suave exterior to the heartless cretin inside.

"How did you meet?"

For the first time, Ingrid smiled, self-deprecating though it was. "I called Sanchez Homes and when I got Dean on the phone, I tried to talk him into a business loan."

Sylvie's eyebrows winged up. "Wow, that's—"

"Dumb. I know now that Dean wasn't the person to talk to, but at the time," she sighed and shook her head, "I was trying to get noticed. I figured that if I landed a big client, I'd get along better with my coworkers. Don't get me wrong, they treat me fine. People around here are nice, but it's hard to make friends, they don't let you in."

Ingrid wasn't the first person to say that about the Puget Sound area, but Sylvie had lived in Keeney her entire life. She'd have to travel a long way to find anonymity.

"So when Dean asked me to have coffee with him, I was ecstatic. And then I met him and…you know." It was a balmy evening, yet Ingrid clutched her mug of tea as if she'd never be warm again. "It really doesn't matter, though. Rent here is really high, and I'm going to have to move back home." She made a resigned face.

Now she was really tugging at Sylvie's heartstrings. How was it that the woman who had literally screwed her boyfriend and given him access to her money made Sylvie feel sorry for her? Something told her that she and Ingrid weren't the only women to be screwed over by Dean.

The server returned carrying a plate of fruit and a bowl of melted chocolate. "It's late, and this won't last until tomorrow," she said, putting the plate down with a smile.

"Thanks. It's not like you to be so nice. What's going on?" Sylvie popped a piece of pineapple in her mouth.

"You did a great job on the drywall in the new bathroom at half the price of the other bid, and I wanted to say thank you. So, eat. And when are you coming back to play ball? We miss you." She turned to Ingrid and smiled. "Hi, I'm Anna. We're on the same softball team when she bothers to show up." She looked Ingrid over assessingly. "You don't play, do you?"

Eyes widening, Ingrid sat up straight. "I do. I made varsity in high school, and our team went to state."

"What year?"

Sylvie pulled the plate of fruit toward her and munched away as Anna and Ingrid carried on. A warmth bubbled up inside her as the two made firm plans to get together, and she made a mental note to tell Ali to ignore her blistering email.

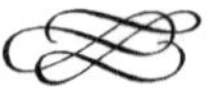

CHAPTER 10

Keeney Field was a misnomer. The vast acreage was a complex within walking distance of downtown Keeney, holding baseball diamonds, soccer and football fields, and a cricket pitch. Close by were an ADA-compliant playground and a skateboard park. Carl was familiar with the skateboard park, having spent many an hour skinning elbows and knees while perfecting his jumps.

Grabbing his glove, he pocketed his keys and phone and headed to the dugout where the KBS Hammers were gathered. He slowed his pace to belie his eagerness but couldn't stop smiling.

KBS didn't have a team when he worked for them years ago, so he had no idea whether they were any good. All he knew was that he'd been asked to play. Tired of spending his evenings either in the gym or on the couch, he'd happily take the position of waterboy.

The slow-pitch beer league was made up of local businesses and a few churches. Ali told him the emphasis was on fun. Running up the score was frowned on, while dancing in the outfield was encouraged.

Carl recognized all but a few players lining the bench.

Unlike the team he'd played on in Olympia, the Hammers were inclusive, and his was not the only dark face in the group. Neither Vincent nor Tomas was present, but their wives were. Hilary was tossing a ball to a blonde woman whose name he couldn't remember, and Fiona sat in a lawn chair between Marcia and Iris on the sidelines.

Born in Lebanon, Ali grew up playing soccer—he still insisted on calling it football—and acted as the team coach. "Here," he said, tossing Carl a T-shirt.

"Thanks." Carl took the shirt and examined the kaleidoscope of bright colors, as well as the large, bedazzled hammer on the back. Grinning, he swapped shirts. Or tried to. "Ali, do you have one that's bigger?" The bright fabric clung to his biceps, strained across his chest, and barely came down to his belly button.

"Nope," Ali smirked. "I guess you're the designated eye candy today."

"Great." A chorus of giggles broke out behind him. At least the belly he was flashing was flat and not flabby.

"Sorry I'm—whoa!" Sylvie stopped short, her eyes crinkling with mirth.

Carl pointed his glove at her. "Not a word," he warned.

"I wouldn't think of it," she replied, rolling her lips between her teeth.

After meeting other members of the team, Carl tossed a ball with Joseph Han, Fiona's brother. The man grinned, but didn't say anything about Carl's shirt, and he soon forgot about it as he got into the easy rhythm of throwing and catching a ball.

The Red Devils were first at bat, and the Hammers took to the field, Carl jogging to a spot between second and third base.

"Yeah, no," Sylvie said. "I play shortstop."

"Oh, my bad." Shortstop was *the* best position, and Carl was good at it. He looked around the infield where players were taking their positions. The only one open was left field. He looked imploringly at Sylvie.

Arms crossed and one hip cocked, she slowly shook her head. "Can it with the puppy-dog eyes. I'm not trading."

Tugging at the too-small shirt, Carl sighed and jogged to the outfield.

❄

It was the second time Ingrid had played with the Hammers, and she was a damn good pitcher. An easy wind-up and the ball floated toward the batter so slowly, it looked like it was going to die before crossing the pitcher's mound. The first two batters struck out, and Sylvie high-fived Anna, who played second base. The only thing better than playing ball on a warm evening was winning.

While being evicted for no fault of her own still stung, Sylvie had settled into her new place nicely. It was roomier, quieter, and a screaming hot deal. The seminary student had moved out of the tiny house, so when Sylvie sat on the back deck, she had tons of privacy. She could sunbathe in the nude if she wanted to. That made her think of Carl's wounded butt, and she looked behind her.

He stood in left field, clearly looking bored. And maybe a little annoyed because he wasn't seeing a lot of action. The too-small T-shirt probably didn't help. If she were feeling generous, she might swap positions later in the game for a few innings. She loved playing shortstop, so it was a big if.

A sharp-featured woman with spiked hair approached the batter's box, swinging the bat like it was a natural extension of her arm. Studying the infield, her gaze seemed to fix on Sylvie, and she spat into the dirt and readied the bat over her shoulder.

Ingrid went into her wind-up and fired the ball. Thwack! The ball fouled off behind third base and hit the ground before Carl could reach it. Sylvie lifted her glove, expecting him to throw it to her, but he sent it directly to Ingrid. His shirt lifted with the movement, exposing more of his firm, dark skin.

"Why does the batter keep giving you a dirty look?" Anna asked.

"Hmm?" Sylvie shifted her focus away from Carl's abdominals and back to the game and the scowling woman in the batter's box. She'd struck out both previous times she'd been at bat, and Sylvie hadn't paid much attention to her. "Oh crap."

"What?"

"That's Lauren. She used to date my sister, and it didn't end well."

That was putting it mildly. Lauren and Cara dated a handful of times while Cara was still studying to be a physiotherapist. Lauren proved to be rather possessive and started questioning Cara's movements, always asking where she was and who she was with. It came to a head the day Lauren made a scene in the Keeney library. She stormed into a conference room where Cara and three other students were prepping for an exam and accused Cara of sleeping around. Cara broke up with her on the spot, and Lauren didn't take it well. She was escorted out of the building by a diminutive librarian whose curls vibrated with indignation.

"But why is she shooting eye daggers at you?"

Sylvie winced. "I may have accidentally covered her windshield with sticky notes."

"Just her windshield?"

"It took longer than I thought, and I ran out."

Anna snorted. "Did they spell out something inappropriate?"

"No. I wish I had thought of that, though."

The bat cracked again, this time sending the ball directly to the pitcher. Caught unprepared, Ingrid bobbled the ball and dropped it before scooping it up and throwing it to first base. Unfortunately, Lauren was already on the bag.

Anna and Sylvie stopped talking to concentrate on the game. The next two batters walked, and Lauren shouldered past Sylvie, wearing an evil grin. The bases were now loaded.

A man emerged from the dugout and approached the batter's box with a cocky strut. As if it were the World Series and he was Cal Raleigh.

"Well, shit," Sylvie said, turning to Anna, "it's Dean."

In the time that they'd been together, he'd never once shown up at one of her games, sneering that the players were washed-up jocks who could barely make it around the bases without an oxygen mask. Was he here tonight simply to torment her? Maybe rub it in her face that he could do whatever the hell he wanted. Because, as far as she knew, Dean hadn't suffered any consequences for his actions. And with his connections, she doubted that he would. He just seemed to keep on winning. Well, that wasn't going to happen today.

"Well, shit," Carl muttered, staring at Dean. Despite the belly-exposing shirt and having to play left field, he'd been having fun, but it looked like that was about to come to an end. His focus was on Sylvie, but he caught Ingrid going rigid on the pitcher's mound and then swinging around to goggle at Sylvie, who'd gone silent. Arms crossed, she shook her head, like she couldn't believe what she was seeing.

Dean must have subbed in for someone because it was the fifth inning, and this was his first time at bat. He took his time, waving to someone in the stands and chatting with the umpire beside home plate. Carl moved closer to the infield as the other outfielders moved back. While Dean looked like he could whack the ball clear into the next zip code, instinct warned Carl that the ball would be headed right at Sylvie.

The Hammers got into position, the runners on base hunkered down and ready to take off. Ingrid fired the ball so fast it whipped past Dean and smacked into the catcher's mitt. "Strike one!" the umpire yelled.

Dean shrugged and smiled. "Nice throw, blondie," he called.

Ignoring him, Ingrid threw the ball low and inside, brushing Dean back from the plate. "Ball!" the umpire shouted.

Dean smiled again. "Good thing I wore a cup tonight. Wouldn't want to damage the family jewels."

The Hammers groaned while chuckles came from the Red Devils' bench.

"If she hits him, he's gonna walk," Carl said.

"If she hits him, I'll buy her a drink," Sylvie said over her shoulder. "A house if she knocks him on his ass."

Ingrid checked over her shoulders for leadoffs, wound up, and fired. Dean hit the ball like he'd made a special request for it.

"Mine!" Sylvie yelled, glove raised and backpedaling into center field.

She wouldn't make it. The ball was moving too fast, and Sylvie was too short. Carl knew that in his soul and figured he had two choices. Hang back and watch the ball sail over her outstretched arm while the Red Devils scored, or grab the ball and face Sylvie's wrath.

His feet were in motion before he consciously made the decision. "Mine!" he yelled and caught the ball moments before Sylvie crashed into his chest.

Her ball cap fell off, and her eyes glittered as she righted herself. "That was mine! You heard me call it."

"Yes, I did," Carl replied evenly. "But we both know you

weren't going to get it." He picked up her cap and brushed off the grass before giving it back to her.

"I could have!"

"Only if you had a springboard. That ball was a good two feet out of your reach."

She wanted to protest. He could see it in the obstinate set of her jaw. Instead, she muttered, "Fine." And then, unexpectedly, "Good save," before jogging to the dugout, hips swaying and ponytail swinging.

Carl followed more slowly, watching Sylvie link arms with Ingrid and walk to the dugout. Unfortunately, he was too slow, and he met up with Dean near third base. He fixed a smile in place and attempted to skirt around him.

But Dean was in a chatty mood and said, "Nice catch. We'd be whipping Hammer ass if you'd left it to Sylvie. I knew she'd go for it. I'm surprised at Blondie, though. I thought she was all looks and no game."

Carl twisted away from the hand Dean raised to slap his back and pitched his voice so that it would carry, "Ingrid's a great pitcher. We're lucky to have her."

He moved to the dugout before Dean could respond, and Ali patted his shoulder. "Good job," he said.

Carl shrugged. "It was an easy catch."

Ali shook his head. "The catch was good, but I meant sticking up for Ingrid. She needed to hear that."

Carl looked toward where Ingrid sat beside Sylvie. Receiving smiles from both women felt better than hitting a home run.

When it was time to hit the field again, Sylvie walked beside him and offered to switch positions. "Thanks," he replied, "but I'm happy backing you up. I wasn't trying to steal your thunder, I just didn't want to watch Dean do a victory lap."

"I appreciate that, and I'm happy to know you have my back."

Her smile wasn't very big when she answered, and he suspected she wasn't referring to playing softball.

CHAPTER 11

oday was the last day he would need supervision before being allowed to work as a contractor all on his own. After weeks of first following Ali around, and then being trailed by another employee, he felt like a kid itching to have the training wheels taken off his bicycle. Propped against the side of the truck, he scrolled through his phone, waiting for Vincent to show up. It reminded him of that day years ago when Iris's son insisted Vincent needed supervising when he went out to work on a customer's home. Carl snickered. Things had sure changed since then.

Scott, his boss at Build Clean, wanted an update. Had Carl made progress with Sanchez Homes?

He was on an unpaid leave of absence and technically wasn't working. And Dean Sanchez gave him the icks. If his treatment of Sylvie wasn't enough, his comments about Ingrid proved he was a sleazeball, and Carl wanted nothing to do with him. Scott could wait.

Carl shoved his phone in his pocket and rolled a pebble beneath his work boot. It was stupid to have agreed to Scott's request, but not being in the Olympia office meant that Carl's chances of getting the Alaska job were diminishing.

And he really wanted it. Not working on the frozen tundra per se. But being in charge of the department. Having people report to him instead of him reporting to others. And the pay hike wasn't anything to laugh at either.

Oddly enough, this gig at KBS would not hurt him. Arriving in Alaska with scuffed work boots and experience using the product—because KBS did carry Clean Wrap— would give him a bit of street cred with the permanent employees.

He stretched and looked to the loading dock to see what was taking Vincent so long, then straightened. "Shit."

Instead of Vincent, Tomas was headed his way. It wasn't a bad thing, just…different. Tomas spent more time as an instructor than he did with clients and preferred it that way. He was quietly competent and a little intimidating. Or was that because Carl was having *thoughts* about Sylvie? Ever since she'd pulled the splinters out of his ass and he'd felt her touch, he couldn't stop thinking about her. It was hard not to because work threw them together more often than not. It wasn't his place, but he wanted to know if she'd gotten her money back. If she was heartbroken over Dean, or if she was ready to move on.

Every time he entered KBS, he looked for her. Perked up when he heard her voice. Every flash of pink made him think of her, and he wondered what color underwear she wore.

Carl met Tomas's glare. Was he a mind reader? Was that why he looked like he was chewing nails?

"Hey," Carl said by way of greeting.

Tomas grunted and climbed into the passenger seat.

"Alrighty then." Carl rounded the truck to the driver's side.

. . .

The first two jobs went smoothly, involving the installation of a garage door opener at one house and the replacement of three fence panels at another. Tomas had stood back, let Carl interact with the clients, and take the lead on everything. Carl was a little jittery at first. Vincent and Ali were talkers and easy to be around. Tomas clearly had something on his mind and spoke only when necessary. But his smile was friendly and his manner easy with the two small children who watched them fix the fence, including letting them each hammer in a nail.

So Carl had relaxed slightly as they got in the truck for the last call of the day. "Where to?" he asked.

Tomas squinted at the clipboard, then thrust it at Carl. "Haven't a clue," he said. "It's handwritten and looks like chicken scratch to me."

When they stopped at a red light, Carl read out the job details and the address, and then headed in the right direction. Keeney wasn't that big, and he didn't need GPS to find the house.

"That's Iris's house," Tomas said.

"Huh," Carl replied. "Wonder why Sylvie isn't going to fix it. She can do plumbing, can't she?"

"Yeah, but why would she?"

"'Cause she lives right upstairs from Iris."

Tomas scowled. "Since when?"

"Since Dean got her evicted."

"What?"

"You didn't know?" He glanced over. The tick in Tomas's jaw told Carl the answer.

"Drive faster," Tomas bit out.

.   .   .

*J*ris chattered away as they repaired her kitchen sink, and they were loading up the truck when a dusty Subaru parked in the driveway. Sylvie waved at them through the windshield, gathered her things, and got out.

Legs wide and hands on his hips, Tomas blocked the stairway leading to her place on the upper floor. "What happened and why am I just finding out now?"

Sylvie sighed and looked at Carl, who raised his hands. "Sorry, I thought he already knew."

"Because you'd do this," Sylvie told Tomas.

"Do what?"

She waved her hand up and down in front of him. "This! Be the overbearing, overprotective big brother who thinks he needs to weigh in on everything."

"That clown got you evicted. Of course, I get to weigh in on that."

Iris emerged from her house, skirted the arguing pair, and walked over to Carl. "What's going on?"

"Tomas didn't know about Dean getting Sylvie evicted. I told him what I knew and—" he gestured toward the standoff between the siblings "—they're having words."

"Ahh." Iris settled against the side of the truck, like she was preparing to be entertained.

"You're not worried?" Carl stared at her. "There could be bloodshed."

Bent at the waist, Tomas spoke so rapidly in Spanish that Carl made out only a few words. Sylvie poked him in the chest. Her words were easier to understand; she clearly wanted him to stay in his lane.

"He needs to get it out of his system," Iris replied. "He's hurt that she didn't tell him herself. But if she had told him when it happened…" She gave Carl a meaningful look.

Carl nodded his understanding. He'd worked with Tomas long enough to know that he cared deeply about the people he was closest to. Dean Sanchez would have had more than a dented car had Tomas known earlier.

Throwing his hands in the air, Tomas declared, "You have shitty taste in men!"

Sylvie scoffed, "Don't lecture me. It's not like you haven't made a bad decision in your life." She crossed her arms and tapped a foot against the pavement. "At least mine didn't cost me five years in jail."

"No. But it got you evicted and cost you three hundred thousand dollars!"

Her face going white, Sylvie flinched and turned away. Carl stepped forward, unsure whether he wanted to comfort Sylvie or kick her brother. Iris held him back, shaking her head.

"Aww, shit!" Tomas scrubbed his face with his hands and sighed. "That was uncalled for. I'm sorry, Sylvie."

He reached out, but she pulled away. He moved closer and put a hand on her head, sliding it down to tug on her ponytail. "You're right. If I'd known when it happened, I would have gone nuclear. It's just…"

She turned to face him, wiping under an eye. "You're overbearing and overprotective?"

"Maybe a little."

She crossed her arms and cocked a hip, sniffling loudly.

"Maybe a lot," Tomas said, spreading his arms wide. "How can I help?"

Sylvie darted forward and face-planted against his chest. "A hug would be nice."

Wrapping his arms around her, Tomas rocked Sylvie back and forth. Looking up, he blinked as if noticing the audience watching their heated argument. Then he said something to Sylvie that made her giggle.

Iris sighed. "Good. See? They'll be fine." She twisted to look up at Carl. "Didn't you and your sister ever get into fights like that?"

"With Mandy? No." His older sister had the easy-going nature of their father and the organized mind of their mother. She usually agreed with everything, and if she didn't, she preferred to present her argument in written form, often accompanied by diagrams and bullet points. The only time Carl ever saw Mandy get worked up about something was when he touched one of her Pokémon cards with his bare hands. Her distress had made him feel like a schmuck. The Ryder family wasn't close and in each other's business the way Sylvie's family was. Which was a relief. Yet, other than texting about Gram, when was the last time he and Mandy talked? He made a mental note to do so soon.

Sylvie pulled back from her brother and moved toward the stairs, saying, "See you later," to Iris and Carl.

Tomas looked at him. "Can you take the truck back? We're done for the day, and I'm going to eat with Sylvie." At Carl's nod, he followed his sister to her apartment.

Iris went into her garden, and Carl stood in the driveway, kind of hoping Sylvie would invite him to stay too. But no, so he pulled out his phone and climbed into the truck. Connecting to the vehicle's Bluetooth, he scrolled through his playlist. Nothing caught his attention, so he went to his contacts instead.

Mandy picked up after the third ring, and he took the long way back to KBS while talking to his sister.

At Carl's request, Sylvie accompanied him to visit his grandmother in the rehab facility to present the sketch of her new apartment with the furniture in place. She didn't think her presence was necessary, but went anyway and sat quietly while Carl explained the need to pare down. Miss Jean was not pleased, insisting that she needed every stick of furniture and knick-knack on her list. Cara, Sylvie's sister, came in to guide Miss Jean through her physiotherapy exercises and studied the sketch. She praised Miss Jean for being forward-thinking and pointed out how much easier it would be to maneuver a walker in an apartment that wasn't cluttered with furniture. That settled the matter, and to Carl's obvious relief, his grandmother agreed.

Professional movers were hired, which made things a little easier on moving day, but ensuring the correct items were taken was a lot of work. Carl again requested that Sylvie be there to help him. Throughout the day, he thanked her more than once, admitting that he couldn't have done it without her. She agreed, which made him laugh.

The first thing unloaded from the truck was Miss Jean's recliner. Once it was positioned to her satisfaction, she settled into it to supervise. After the movers left, Sylvie stayed behind to help Carl hang pictures and unpack boxes, enjoying the stories Miss Jean told about her family.

They were finishing up as another resident was moving in across the hall. It was not going well, and the woman's complaints were clearly audible through the open door.

Miss Jean shook her head. "That's Inez Olson, and she is not happy to be here," she said in a low voice. "She wanted to stay in her home, but she can't handle the front steps, and because the bathroom door is too narrow, she couldn't get her walker inside, so she's fallen a lot."

"And she insisted on bringing *all* her furniture," she added, rolling her eyes.

Images of the unhappy woman stayed in Sylvie's thoughts as she returned home and saw Iris puttering in her backyard. In her late sixties, she'd been smart to move into the lower level of her house before stairs became an issue for her.

"How did the move go?" Iris asked, removing her gardening gloves.

"Really well. Miss Jean seems very happy."

"Good. I'm glad you were there to help."

"The movers did all the work, I just helped unpack," Sylvie replied.

Iris pursed her lips. "I think you did more than that. Carl would have been lost without you, so thank you for stepping up."

"It wasn't a hardship," Sylvie said truthfully. She'd enjoyed being with him. He'd consulted with her, instead of telling her what to do, didn't assume she couldn't do something simply because she was smaller and female, and never condescended. Having met his grandmother, she understood where that came from, but appreciated it, nonetheless.

When they were finally finished in Miss Jean's new apartment, he'd insisted on walking her to her car and gave her a quick, sweaty hug. "I owe you big time," he'd said with a tired smile.

"No, you don't. I know it was you who *accidentally* damaged my bed and had it replaced. I think we're even."

He grinned. "Not even close."

The image of Carl walking back into Cascades Lodge prompted Sylvie to ask, "Iris, this is going to sound like a weird question, but how long do you want to live in this house?"

"That is weird," Iris said.

Both women turned to face the house. Beneath the deck, an eight-foot-wide patio ran the length of the house. Outdoor furniture and flowerpots were arranged in an inviting seating area. Unlike Sylvie's French doors, Iris's entryway was a single, wide, solid door. Not big enough to be called a ramp, there was a slight lip between the patio and the bottom of the door, something easily navigated by someone with mobility issues.

"I thought about that when Vincent did the remodel for me, so we made it accessible. There's no carpeting, and the entries and halls are quite wide. I've got grab bars in the bathroom, and if I need to hire a caregiver, they could stay in the tiny house."

"You were really thinking ahead," Sylvie said.

Iris swept her arms out. "I love my home, and I want to stay here as long as I can, so it made sense to make those modifications before I needed them. Why did you ask?"

"I think I want to revise my plan for flipping houses." She'd received a call from Andrea at the bank, informing her that her money was back in her account, and she had almost cried at the good news.

"How so?"

Sylvie explained about Inez Olson's predicament and said, "I want to buy ranch-style homes and make them more accessible."

"That's not cheap, and it's a niche market."

Sylvie nodded. "True, but I think there is a market for it."

Iris gave her an assessing look and led the way to the patio. "I do some of my best thinking here," she said, settling into a chair.

Sylvie joined her, gripping her knees to keep them from bouncing. "Anyone with accessibility issues would be the market, and I don't just mean older people. This area has a lot of single-level homes that were built long ago and are being bought up to be replaced by tall, narrow houses that don't work for wheelchairs and walkers."

Iris nodded slowly. "That's true. Those new houses two blocks over wouldn't work for anyone who can't do stairs. Do you have a house in mind? That duplex you were looking at wouldn't fit the bill."

"I'm thinking about Miss Jean's house. It hasn't gone on the market yet, and I know the asking price will be higher than for the duplex because her house is in good shape and in a great neighborhood. However, I'm fairly certain I can qualify for a mortgage. I know it needs some repairs before they can sell it, so I've got time to get my ducks in a row."

Iris slapped her thighs. "I think it's an excellent idea and a perfect fit for Tomas."

"Oh, I don't think so. Work with my brother? I'd rather have a root canal." No, when she thought about working alongside someone else, it was Carl's image that came to mind.

few days later, Sylvie met with Miss Jean and Carl. Miss Jean listened in silence, nodding occasionally in what Sylvie hoped was approval. Carl crossed his arms and asked, "Why go to so much trouble? A simple flip wouldn't take nearly as long, and your profit margin would be greater."

"Carl," Miss Jean scolded him, "that is none of our business. I think it's a wonderful idea, and she doesn't have to justify herself."

"No, ma'am," Sylvie replied. "It's a fair question because my offer is lower than what you'd receive if you sold your house on the open market. You'd be taking a chance on me, and Carl is simply looking out for your best interests."

She peered at her grandson over her glasses. "Is that correct?"

Carl grinned and shrugged. "I'd certainly look better if that were my reasoning. Seriously, though, it's curiosity. It's an ambitious project and you'd be taking a risk. You think there's a market without knowing that for a fact. So why not play it safe?"

Thinking about how to answer, Sylvie sat back and stared at the framed photographs that hung above Miss Jean's couch. In one was a photo of Carl, wearing a logoed polo shirt and leaning against a sign that read "Build Clean." She assumed that the building behind him was the company's corporate headquarters.

"The company you work for uses environmentally

friendly, sustainable practices to manufacture environmentally friendly products. It takes longer, costs more to make, and they have to charge higher prices than their competition. From a profit standpoint, *that* doesn't make sense. Yet they do it anyway, and have been very successful despite not playing it safe."

She gestured toward Miss Jean's front door. "I got this idea because Mrs. Olson across the hall wanted to grow old in her home and wasn't able to do so. Builders don't think about that. Unless specifically asked, they don't widen doorways, or lower countertops or install ramps. Miss Jean, your house needs to be updated before it can be sold, and I think the layout is perfect for someone with accessibility issues. If I do it right, your house will be perfect for someone who needs accommodations."

She blew out a breath. "I'm not saying this well, but I believe everyone deserves a place to live that fits them, not the other way around. And I'm willing to settle for a smaller profit if I can help make that happen. Does that make sense?"

Miss Jean and Carl shared a look, then Miss Jean patted Sylvie's hand. "Perfectly, dear, now where do I sign?"

CHAPTER 12

The loading dock was a mess of epic proportions. An inattentive forklift driver had pierced a pallet full of sand, which cascaded all over the floor. Then they backed the forklift into a stack of terra cotta containers that toppled and shattered. Ali would have been pulling his hair out if he had any, as fingers pointed left, right, and center.

Sylvie bit her lip and sidled over to where Carl stood against the tailgate of a loaded pickup. "So, is now a good time to ask Ali about inventory loss?"

"Only if you want your head bitten off." Carl swigged from his water bottle. "How've you been?"

His gaze roved over her, and she froze, expecting a cutting remark about her appearance. Dean had always complained about her work clothes. She wasn't required to wear the KBS polo shirt and khakis, but they made getting dressed one less thing to think about in the morning. Dean had spent more time in front of the mirror than she did and didn't understand her logic.

However, ever since the softball game, she'd wanted Carl to notice her. The Red Devils beat the Hammers by 4-3, which was fine because Dean hadn't made it on base once. It would have been more satisfying to have seen him knocked unconscious by a ball to the head, but she'd take her wins where she could get them.

The team had gone to a bar after the game for drinks and munchies, and it was good to see Ingrid blossom under all the attention. Sylvie even heard her and Anna making plans to get pedicures together. Carl's own shirt had been mysteriously lost, and he'd worn the ridiculously small team shirt to the bar. Sylvie's prank backfired, though, because not only did Carl wear the shirt without complaint, but he also drew a lot of attention. A lot of attention that lingered on his really, really nice arms and flat belly. He sat across from Sylvie, and every time he moved, his belly button winked at her. Napkins piled up in front of Carl, with names and phone numbers on them, and Sylvie was tempted to accidentally spill her drink on them.

So, today, she'd swapped her shapeless cargo pants for slim-fitting chinos and a KBS button-down in a lighter shade of blue, and gold hoop earrings. Choosing her footwear had been a problem. KBS required employees to wear closed-toed shoes, and because she was all over the building and lumber yard, Sylvie usually wore work boots. Today, she'd opted for pink suede sneakers. Carl smiled and pointed his water bottle at her shoes. "Cute," he said, offering her the bottle.

The heat of her blush added to the heat of the day, and she accepted the water bottle appreciatively, pressing it against the back of her neck rather than taking a drink. Her phone rang, and her heart rate kicked up when she saw the name. "It's the bank," she told Carl.

"You've got this," Carl said, his eyes lighting up.

She moved away from the noise of the loading dock and pressed up against the side of the building. "Hello," she said brightly. The plans she'd drawn up for renovating the duplex weren't completely useless. There were definite modifications to be made, but they'd provided a good starting point, and Miss Jean wasn't in a hurry to sell, so Sylvie had been able to take her time formulating a budget.

"Sylvie? It's Andrea. We've reviewed your mortgage application and agreed that what you intend is a sound investment."

She felt a presence behind her and turned to find Carl watching her, eyebrows raised inquiringly. She gave him a thumbs up, and he lifted a hand for a high five.

"However, given the recent activity in your account, the bank feels that the risk is too high and has declined your application."

Rather than slapping Carl's hand, Sylvie clutched it. "But that wasn't my fault!"

"I know, and I brought that up, but they wouldn't budge."

The smile fell from Carl's face, and he stepped closer, preventing anyone on the loading dock from being able to see her. She blinked back tears as Andrea continued talking in a sympathetic tone, but it didn't really matter what she said; the answer was still no. Sylvie murmured a goodbye and signed off.

"I didn't get it," she said in a quavering voice. She'd put in hours on her proposal, writing and rewriting her business plan, filling out the forms, and checking them over. And more hours dreaming and planning how she'd transform Miss Jean's house. Now she was back at square one. There were other banks, but if word got around she'd been rejected, would she ever get her business off the ground? Waves of self-pity rolled over her, and she fought back the tears.

Carl gathered her close and pressed her head against his chest, not saying a word as she sobbed against his shirt.

. . .

arrying two milkshakes, Carl returned from Duwamish Drive-In's order window and climbed into the truck. "Your choice," he said. "Chocolate or strawberry."

She took the strawberry with a murmured "thank you" and slurped up the cold, sugary goodness.

In the bright sunshine, life went on all around them, unaware of Sylvie's shattered dreams. Parents fed their children French fries at tables shaded by brightly colored umbrellas while a group of high school kids jostled each other in the back parking lot. The girls in the briefest clothing possible, and the boys in baggy jeans and baggy shirts. Marcia had commented once that the boys' shaggy hairstyles made them look like alpacas, and Sylvie couldn't get that image out of her head.

"What did the bank say?" Without questioning her, Carl had bundled her into the truck when she couldn't stop crying, spoken to Ali, and driven off from KBS.

"They think I'm too high of a risk because of the *recent activity*," Sylvie put air quotes around the words, "in my account. But I am welcome to reapply with a cosigner."

"Thank you, Dean Sanchez," she muttered and sucked back her milkshake.

"What do you mean?"

"I had qualified for a mortgage, but then Dean accessed— his word, not mine—my money, and the original house I wanted to buy sold before I could get my money back."

Carl looked pained and uncomfortable, and Sylvie realized how much she whined at him. If she kept up with the pity parties, pretty soon, he'd turn and run away whenever he saw her.

"Let's talk about something else," she said. "How much longer will you be in Keeney?"

"Another six weeks or so. It depends."

"On what?"

"I requested a ninety-day leave of absence, but that was before I knew that Gram had congestive heart failure." He didn't look at her as he sipped his milkshake. "Build Clean isn't happy, but I want more time because I don't want to leave her alone. So I won't take off until my parents are back and they can keep an eye on her."

He was easy to talk to, and she'd been so caught up in the fallout from Dean that she'd forgotten why he'd returned to Keeney. "Miss Jean seems to be doing alright."

Carl bobbed his head. "She is. She's a tough old bird. I'm just having a hard time wrapping my head around the whole heart thing because it's not going to get better. And for some reason, no one in my family thought to tell me about it. I think the only reason they did was because there's work to be done and I'm the only one available to do it." His voice was filled with bitterness. "Your parents probably drive you nuts at times, but it must be nice to have someone call just to shoot the shit and not because there's been a crisis."

She'd never really thought about it, but it was true. A day didn't go by that she didn't hear from Cara or her mother, even if it was only a silly meme. "They get along now, but there was a time when Tomas and my dad barely spoke to each other. Tomas was a hot head when he was younger."

"Why does that not surprise me?" Carl muttered.

"Right?" Sylvie grinned. "He got into trouble in school, and Dad wouldn't put up with it, so family dinners were pretty tense. And it didn't help matters when Dad got Tomas arrested."

Carl whipped his head around. "You're kidding."

"Nope. But if you want the details, you're gonna have to ask Tomas."

He smirked. "Yeah, like that's gonna happen."

It was nice to listen to him for a change, cheer him up.

Even if it was at her brother's expense.

Carl gestured toward the kids in the back parking lot. "Someone's gonna get hurt."

She followed his gaze and spotted a small form huddled in an abandoned shopping cart, clinging to the sides as another kid swung the cart around in circles. The shopping cart was let go and careened wildly across the asphalt, crashing into a cement retaining wall to uproarious laughter.

Sylvie and Carl were out of the truck, their doors slamming simultaneously like they'd practiced.

"Oy," Carl shouted. Wearing dark glasses and no longer smiling, the easy-going man who doled out hugs and bought her ice cream and milkshakes was transformed into an intimidating avenger with one word.

The kids scattered like cockroaches before a flashlight, but not before Carl snagged a mop-headed boy by the back of the shirt.

The girl in the shopping cart was clambering to her feet when Sylvie reached her. "Careful," she said, taking the girl's hands and helping her out. "You okay?"

Glassy-eyed and white-faced, the girl stared at Sylvie. She made a choking sound, turned her head, and threw up, narrowly missing Sylvie's shoes.

The back door of the drive-in burst open, and a tiny, old woman, swathed in an apron and brandishing a garden hose, stepped out. "Get the hell out of here! I've told you kids—"

Carl removed his sunglasses and smiled down at the woman. "Hi, Mrs. Wong."

The proprietor of Keeney's only drive-in restaurant peered up at him. "Carl?"

"Yep. It's me. How ya doing?"

Still holding the hose, Mrs. Wong crossed her arms and nodded. "Good, good. Can't complain. How's your grandmother? I heard she broke her hip."

"It's slow, but she's getting better."

"Good. You let her know I said hi."

The mop-headed boy looked up at Carl. "Can I go now?"

"Nope," Carl replied, then asked Sylvie, "Is she okay?"

A little color had returned to the girl's face, and she wiped her face with the back of her hand before nodding.

"Hi, Mrs. Wong," Sylvie said, leading the girl toward the others.

Mrs. Wong studied her and shook her head. "Sorry, hun. I know you're one of Louisa's girls, but I can't remember your name."

"I'm Sylvie."

"Right. And who do you have here?"

"Not sure," Sylvie answered. "That one," she pointed at the boy, "was part of a group whirling this one," she indicated the girl, "around in the shopping cart, and then let it crash into the wall."

"Again? Did she vomit?"

Sylvie gestured toward the splattered mess steaming on the hot pavement. "Yep."

Mrs. Wong pointed at the girl. "You bring me the cart."

"And you," she handed the hose to the boy, "clean up the mess."

Watching the teens hurry off to do as told, Sylvie asked Mrs. Wong, "Do they do that a lot?"

"Only when the dishwasher leaves my cart outside. They said it's for a TikTok challenge." Seeing Sylvie's bewildered look, she added. "I know. Stupid."

Gesturing to a camera mounted above the back door, she said, "When I see them out here, I threaten them with the hose. I've only had to use it once."

The boy returned the hose to Mrs. Wong and asked, "Now, can we go?"

"Yeah. Get out of here."

The boy grabbed the girl's hand and they hurried off.

Shaking her head, Mrs. Wong said, "If that's what dating

looks like these days, I don't know what the world is coming to."

She grabbed the cart, and Carl held the door open for her. "You two want anything? On the house for my favorite ex-dishwasher." She winked at Carl. "You never left the cart outside."

His dark cheeks turning red, Carl said, "Thanks, Mrs. Wong, but we need to get going."

"All right then, but don't be a stranger."

They returned to the truck, and Sylvie grabbed her milkshake, dropping it in a nearby trash can. "After seeing that, I don't think I want this anymore."

Carl did the same, saying, "Don't blame you. It's a real shame, though, because I haven't had one of these in years."

"They don't make milkshakes in the big city?" Sylvie teased.

"Not as good as these. I used to have one every night after I got off work."

"How long did you work here?"

"Just for the summer after I graduated from high school." Carl grinned. "The girl I had a crush on worked here. Unfortunately, my first day was her last day. So my plan to get close to her was a bust."

"And no one else fell for your devastating good looks?"

He circled his face with one hand. "This devastatingly handsome face was covered in pimples, and I ended each shift smelling like a French fry. Gram insisted I throw my clothes in the wash and have a shower as soon as I got home. There was no action to be had that summer."

Sylvie laughed with him as he started the truck. For a moment, she fantasized about a relationship with Carl. No doubt he'd be as generous in bed as he was in his daily life, and she imagined hours spent exploring each other. As if he knew she was thinking about him, he turned toward her. His wide mouth was turned up in a slight smile, and dark glasses covered his eyes. She couldn't read his expression, and she donned her own sunglasses to prevent him from reading hers.

The loading dock was less chaotic when they pulled into the KBS lot. The forklift was parked off to the side, and the driver and another employee were cleaning up the mess. Ali spotted them and waved, looking less like he was going to have a coronary.

Carl parked the truck and turned to Sylvie. "Listen," he said, removing his glasses. "I know you wanted to buy Gram's house outright, but would you consider Gram hiring you to fix it up before she puts it on the market? We talked about it after you left, and even if *you* don't buy the house first, Gram wants to renovate it using your ideas."

"The renovations will cost more if you make the house accessible."

"We know."

"And the profit margin will be lower."

"We know," he said again. "But we have to hire someone, so why not you?"

"That's...but I've never done this before and I...really?" she squeaked, a bubble of hope rising up inside her.

One hand draped over the steering wheel, he reached over to tug lightly on her ponytail. "Really. I'll be your helper. You can order me around and everything."

She refrained from leaping across the console and smothering him in grateful kisses. Instead, she slumped against the door, grinning from ear to ear. "You're on."

CHAPTER 13

$\mathcal{C}$arl stared at the email, trying to formulate a response to his boss's question: How is it going with Sanchez Homes?

Good was his honest answer. If he knew nothing about Dean's character, he'd pursue the contract with enthusiasm. However…

He drank his coffee and stared out into the backyard, where the neighbor kid was fighting with the lawnmower. Carl had cut the lawn once and been roundly scolded by Gram for doing so. Apparently, the kid—she'd told him his name, but Carl couldn't remember—was saving up to buy an e-bike, and Gram was a regular client. Not a surprise, years ago she'd paid Carl to cut the grass and wash her car when he wanted a new skateboard. Gram didn't believe in handouts, but was willing to pay for inexpert services.

He turned away from the window and eyed the leftover furniture.

Now that Gram was settled, the next order of business was to have an "estate sale," which was a grand way of inviting strangers into your home to poke at your stuff and offer peanuts for it, or so Marcia told him. The sale was scheduled for tomorrow, with all proceeds going to a United Methodist women's ministry. The church ladies would do everything, including holding a bake sale on the front lawn for the bargain hunters. All Carl had to do was move the few things that weren't for sale into the garage and label them accordingly. He'd wondered fleetingly if Sylvie would come, but there was no reason for her to be there. In fact, Carl didn't even need to be there, which was a relief and probably the reason Gram had opted not to be present. It would be difficult to watch memories in the form of her possessions march out the door.

So, except for answering the email, he had nothing to do. His job for today at KBS had been rescheduled, everything was set for tomorrow's sale, and he couldn't even mow the freaking grass.

Without mentioning Dean by name, Carl dashed off an email stating that things were looking good with Sanchez Homes, telling himself it was the truth. But it didn't feel good because what Dean had done to Sylvie was wrong on so many levels. Even though Sylvie's money had been returned to her, not getting a mortgage was the result of Dean's underhanded behavior.

The image of Sylvie's shattered expression when she'd received the news flashed through his mind. Holding her and then getting her away from prying eyes was the right thing to do. Yet, a part of him wished he could do more than let her cry on his shoulder and buy her a milkshake. It had been on the tip of his tongue to tell her about Build Clean and Sanchez Homes, but he'd been a coward. Like doing business with Dean's family's company was choosing the wrong side. In the end, he'd kept quiet, knowing there was a good chance Sylvie would never find out, and even if she did, Carl would be up in Alaska, far away from her wrath.

Restless, he grabbed his workout gear and headed to the gym, an affiliate of the one he belonged to in Olympia. He'd sneered the first time he entered, disappointed at the lack of a sauna and cold plunge bath. But when he'd thought about it, he realized that even though he paid extra for the amenities, he'd never used them. And he grudgingly had to admit that the Keeney gym had a better selection of smoothies at half the cost.

An hour later, he racked the weights and took a swig from his water bottle. Working up a sweat and zoning out to a heavy metal playlist had been just the thing. He'd timed it well, finishing as the weight room began to fill up with the lunchtime crowd. A mixture of men and women in varying stages of fitness and a variety of workout wear. Some were dressed like Carl, in utilitarian shorts and shirts, while others wore clothes designed for showing off and being seen. A guy in a close-fitting shirt with the sleeves cut off, biceps on display, was chatting up a woman on an elliptical machine. Carl's chuckle turned into a cough when he realized it was Dean, who'd spotted Carl and was headed his way.

"Hey man, good to see you. Want to spot me?" He indicated a weight bench that was set up for chest presses.

Carl popped an earbud out and returned his smile. "Sorry, dude, I'm headed out. I've got to…" What? Go somewhere? Save the world? His mind churned, looking for a suitable excuse. His phone dinged audibly. *Thank Christ.* Making a face, he waved it at Dean and headed to the exit at a brisk pace. "I'll catch you another time," he called over his shoulder and engaged the call without looking at the screen. "This is Carl."

It was Sylvie. "Where are you? Get to KBS as quick as you can!"

"What? Are you okay?" The initial warmth at the sound of her voice dissipated as her anxious tone took hold. He lengthened his stride to get to his car faster, then slowed down when she laughed lightly.

"I'm fine. Ali is going to propose to Marcia."

"That's all? I thought the building was burning down."

"*That's all?* The man is a total wreck. He asked Vincent for permission to marry his mother." She sighed. "It's so sweet. Now hurry!"

It was easy to figure out where the proposal would take place because a crowd had gathered near the classroom. What used to be a storage area had been converted into a teaching space with twelve workbenches facing a raised platform. Years ago, Carl had been present for the first class Tomas taught on home repair. All of three people had shown up to that one. Now there was a waiting list for the free classes, especially the ones taught in Spanish.

"Finally!" Sylvie hurried over and grabbed his arm, then quickly released it, crinkling her nose. "Ooh. You're all sweaty."

"Yeah. I was at the gym," he grumbled, following her to the crowded doorway.

"Dammit. I've lost my spot." Sylvie bounced on her toes, trying to see over the people in front of her.

"Do you really want to watch this?"

She looked at him like he was an idiot. "Uh, yeah. Don't you?"

Instead of answering, he squatted and pointed to his shoulders. "Climb on."

Sylvie's eyes lit up. "Really?" She was in motion before Carl could respond, swinging one leg, and then the other over his shoulders.

When she was in place, he grabbed her knees and stood.

"This is so much better. Can you see too?"

"Yeah." It was mostly women in front of him, none of whom were tall enough to block his view, and Ali was clearly visible through the double glass doors.

Dressed in a suit and tie and pacing beside the workbenches, Ali mopped his bald head and clutched a bouquet of red roses in his meaty fist.

"He really asked Vincent for permission?"

"Um-hmm. I wasn't there, but I heard about it from Hilary."

"That seems so…old-fashioned." Carl hadn't dated anyone long enough to meet their family, and couldn't imagine asking their family for permission to marry them. Maybe Ali did it because he'd been in Vincent's life for many years and had been somewhat of a father figure.

"Agreed," Sylvie said. Her thigh muscles tightened, and she briefly held his forehead before letting go.

He gripped her knees more firmly. "You alright up there?"

"I'm okay. You?"

A girl sitting on his shoulders wasn't a regular occurrence. But it was Sylvie, and somehow, it just felt right. "I'm fine." And he was. The restlessness that had been dogging him all day had dissipated. He was with someone who wanted to include him in a moment that was meaningful to people. People, he now realized, he cared a great deal about.

In the time he'd been away from Keeney, he'd been invited out for drinks or to play ball. He had coworkers and acquaintances, as well as people at the gym who'd spot for him. But he'd never had someone who'd call and say, "Come see this." He squeezed Sylvie's knee again, liking the feel of her weight on him. Today, she wore a sleeveless top and tailored shorts outfit that highlighted her firm arms and solid thighs. Her golden skin felt satiny smooth, and he enjoyed the play of muscles beneath his hands. He reined in the urge to glide his hands up and down her legs, staring at Ali instead.

Ali jerked to a halt as Vincent and Hilary entered from the back of the room, holding a blindfolded Marcia between them. They let her go, and Marcia whipped off the blindfold. She took a step back, her hands flying up to cover her mouth.

Ali went down on one knee, holding out a ring box, and the watching crowd sighed as one.

Hearing a sniffle, Carl craned his neck to peer up at Sylvie. Hands clasped, she was grinning and crying simultaneously. Carl shook his head. He'd never understand women.

Marcia threw herself at Ali, and they tumbled to the floor, out of sight behind the workbench. Vincent and Hilary assisted them to stand, and it turned into a group hug.

The people around Carl grinned and chuckled, slowly drifting away until it was just him and Sylvie. He knelt and put his hands on her waist to help her down. She took his hands to steady herself, then turned to face him. "Thanks," she said, eyes sparkling through her tears.

Still on his knees and holding her hands, Carl smiled up at her. It was hard not to when she looked so happy.

He was about to pull her in for a hug when a gruff voice came from behind him. "Is there something I should know about?"

Carl twisted to see a scowling Tomas as Sylvie burst out in laughter.

"Yes," she replied. "Carl just asked me to…" Tomas's glower intensified as Sylvie paused dramatically. "Teach him how to use a reciprocating saw."

She let loose a delighted laugh and danced over to her brother. "Gotcha!"

His lips twitched, and he stalked off, muttering something about Sylvie giving him gray hair.

"For the record," Carl said as he stood to tower over her, "I do know how to use a reciprocating saw."

"I'm sure you do," she replied and poked him in the chest. "But I bet I'm better at it."

There wasn't much left after the crowds had been and gone from yesterday's estate sale, mostly mismatched crockery and kitchen utensils. The church ladies were thrilled with the proceeds and had happily tidied up after the event.

"You okay, Gram?"

Pushing her walker, she made a slow circuit of her house, now empty except for the few pieces of furniture Carl was using.

"Yes," she said. "There have been a lot of memories made in this house, but it's time to let it go. Unless, that is," she eyed him over her glasses, "you want to live here."

"I don't think so."

"Suit yourself."

He followed her to the kitchen table, shuddering at the idea of being trapped in the small town. Thank God Gram was now settled in her suite at the assisted living facility, and it wouldn't be long before he'd move on.

"So," Gram said, easing into a chair, "show me your plans."

"You know they're Sylvie's," Carl explained, laying out the drawings he'd worked on with her. It really hadn't been work. Her plans had been detailed, but he had more experience using the CAD program and had refined them for her. Her excitement was palpable, and he was truly looking forward to working with her.

"Remind me how you know her."

"She's a..." A friend? A coworker? Someone who made him smile every time he thought about her? "She works at KBS. Her sister Cara is your physiotherapist."

"She's very smart. It seems that houses are being built tall and narrow around here. I understand that you can get more houses into a smaller space that way, but stairs don't work for everyone." Gram traced a finger over the sketch of the ramp leading to the front door.

"That's why builders are installing elevators in homes."

Gram eyed him like that was foolishness. "You know, someone who wanted to make a business of retrofitting homes for accessibility could make a tidy living around here."

Carl recognized the hint for what it was. "Ripping up moldy carpet and replacing bad wiring and old plumbing to bring houses up to code? No thanks. Give me a clean, fresh slate any day."

Gram straightened and jutted out her chin. "Are you telling me that you'd rather level this house? That the house where I all but raised you isn't worth the work?"

"No, Gram, that's not what I'm saying," Carl sputtered.

"Then what are you saying?"

Carl stared wildly around him. "It's just…not what I want to do."

"What *do* you want to do?"

He searched for a way to explain his situation. "While I'm here in Keeney, Build Clean wants me to get close to Sanchez Homes, get them to buy our building wrap. It would be a big deal and go a long way toward me getting the job in Alaska."

"I can see why. Sanchez Homes is a large company, and from what I understand, it has a reputation for quality work. Is there a problem? Will they not talk to you?"

"No. It's going well. They like us, they like our product. I think they'll sign."

"So what's the problem?" Gram's sparse eyebrows came together in a frown.

The image of Sylvie wiping away tears came to mind. "I don't feel good about one of their employees. He didn't do anything to me, and he hasn't done anything illegal, but he… uses people." That was probably the politest way to describe Dean's actions.

"Sweetheart, that's about 50 percent of the population."

Carl blew out a sigh. His grandmother wasn't wrong. "The thing is, I feel like I need to take a shower after every time I talk to the guy, and he really did a number on a friend, but my boss isn't going to care. If I don't make this deal, it could take me out of the running for the Alaska job."

"Does your friend know about the deal?"

His gaze drifted down to the drawings on the table. "No."

"Why not?"

He shrugged. "It's never come up."

"How do you think it will go over if your friend finds out on their own?"

"Not well."

"And will you be able to live with yourself if you don't say anything about this guy? You can't control Build Clean's response, but if they are truly a reputable company, they will appreciate the warning. And maybe you should talk to the head of Sanchez Homes."

"Do I have to?" he grumbled, only half in jest.

Gram peered over the top of her glasses. "Am I supposed to answer that?"

"No."

She patted his hand and pointed at the plans. "Now tell me what your role is going to be in this project, aside from pulling up moldy carpeting and bad plumbing."

After walking Gram through the plans and making notes for Sylvie on the questions he couldn't answer, Carl took his grandmother back to Cascades.

Pushing her walker down the hall, she said, "Sweetheart, you're twenty-two—"

"Twenty-four."

She ignored the interruption. "Your life is not set in stone. When you were five, you wanted to drive a garbage truck. When you were ten, you wanted to play professional basketball. When you were sixteen, it was skateboarding."

"Yeah. What are you getting at?"

"Did you know I once worked on a cruise ship?" He shook his head, and she continued, "I used to think that I would always be an OR nurse, but I needed to get away after your grandfather died, so I took a nursing contract and worked on small ships in the Mediterranean. After a year, I came home and returned to nursing at Keeney Hospital, but in a different department. And I changed departments again two years later."

She unlocked the door to her suite and turned around to smile up at him. "That's a long way of saying that you can do different things. Just like there are different paths in nursing, there are different paths in building. Test them out. Try things before you dismiss them."

Back in his truck, he looked at the jobs Ali had lined up for him the next day. Both were consultation appointments with the homeowners. One was to build deck furniture using wood from a tree they'd had removed. Another was designing a backyard playhouse for a child with mobility issues. His mind whirling with ideas, he drove off, wondering if Ali and Gram were conspiring to keep him in Keeney.

CHAPTER 14

Carl studied the sign, Happy Faces Daycare, and the neat house set back from the street. Tiny heads bobbed up and down in the front window, and the woman who appeared behind them waved at Carl. He waved in return, backed the truck into the driveway beside the neat stack of lumber, and looked over his notes.

Jasminder Singh ran a daycare out of her home and wanted an addition off the back. It would be a covered play area with retractable walls, skylights, and a bathroom.

Piece of cake. He would be working with Vincent and Tomas, the first time the trio had been together on a project in years, and he could already hear the wisecracks from Vincent and see the smirks on Tomas's face. But he could hold his own and had a few jokes of his own in his back pocket.

Seeing them arrive, Carl climbed out of the truck, ready to start the day and happy to be working outside. He pulled the blue tarp off the lumber and swore.

"Uh uh uh," Vincent chided, striding up the driveway. "Little people with big ears don't need to hear that kind of talk."

"Yeah? Well look at this." Carl stepped back and swept his arm across the lumber.

"What's the prob—oh shit." Tomas stopped, braced his hands on his hips, and scowled. First at the lumber, then at the others.

"Ingrid," all three of them muttered.

The newest employee at KBS was eager, hardworking, and great with customers, but not so great with measurements, apparently. Instead of a pallet of 2x4x96" pieces of wood, they'd received 2x4x100". Each piece of wood intended for upright supports would need to be trimmed by four inches. Not the end of the world, but a tedious process that would add time to the project.

A gaggle of children dressed in hard hats and tool belts erupted from the house and swarmed the men, yelling loudly. A whistle pierced the air, and they went silent.

"Sorry about that." Jasminder Singh, a fiftyish woman in sneakers and a sari, hustled after them. "They're a little excited."

A tiny girl with pink beads anchoring her black braids pushed back her hard hat to look up at Carl. "Hi. I brought my hammer. Want to see it?" She wrestled a pink plastic hammer out of her tool belt and held it up proudly.

"That's very cool," he said.

Not to be outdone, the four other children pulled out their own tools and waved them in the air for inspection, clamoring for his attention.

"It's gonna be a long day," Vincent said behind him.

Two hours later, the children sat in a circle, each sanding the edges off a block of wood. In the middle of the group was a pile of squares and rectangles ready to be sanded. All the pieces had originated from the too-long 2x4s that Tomas trimmed to the correct size.

"Bloody genius," Vincent said, toasting Carl with his water bottle.

"That would be me," Carl preened.

Tomas grunted.

"I heard a rumor Sylvie's flipping your grandmother's house," Vincent said.

"Something like that," Carl replied. "Gram hired her to rehab the house and make it wheelchair accessible. Sylvie thinks there's a good market for it."

"She went through the Keeney Builds program when she started working for Hilary and was our best student. Even if she and Tomas argued all the time." Vincent grinned, elbowing Tomas. While Carl was in college studying general contracting and interning under Vincent at KBS, the Keeney Builds program—a joint venture between the college, KBS, and Keeney Works, a local nonprofit—was started. It was designed for people who were interested in the trades but had obstacles to overcome, including spotty employment records, prison sentences, and incomplete educations. Vincent and Tomas had been the first instructors.

Vincent counted off on his fingers. "What kind of screws to use. The wattage of light bulbs. If the sky was blue. You name it, they argued about it."

Tomas scowled.

"And she was usually right," Vincent added.

Tomas's scowl turned into a smile. "She's really smart, and I bet she's got some great ideas for your grandmother's house. How come you're not taking the lead?"

"I've been working in sales lately and haven't been as hands-on as Sylvie."

"Just so long as you're not 'hands on' with Sylvie," Tomas said.

Vincent pointed his water bottle at him. "I wouldn't get involved if I were you. They're both adults."

"Yeah? Well this adult is headed to Alaska soon. My sister just got screwed over by one guy. She doesn't need that again."

"Yeah? Well what makes you think Carl would—"

Carl stepped between the friends who were standing nose to nose. "Guys, bring it down a notch. You're scaring the kids."

Five little faces stared wide-eyed at the men. Tomas stepped away from Vincent, relaxing his posture. Vincent gave them a sheepish wave.

Carl approached the kids and squatted down to their level. "They're really not fighting. It's just that, sometimes, friends get really loud when they have different opinions," he said. "Does that ever happen to you?"

Five heads nodded.

"What do you do?" he asked.

The little girl with pink beads said, "Mrs. Singh makes us shake hands."

Six faces stared expectantly at Tomas and Vincent.

Tomas and Vincent stared back, and then at each other. Their hands went out, and the handshake turned into a back slap and a chest bump.

Carl shot them a smug grin as he returned. "I'm thinking of going into mediation. What do you think?"

"Asshat," Tomas grumbled.

By the end of the day, they'd managed to put up the support beams and frame two walls. As they were packing up to leave, Carl handed out carpenter pencils to the kids, who then decorated the wood under the watchful eye of Mrs. Singh's assistant.

Tomas left to take Fiona to a prenatal check-up, so Vincent caught a ride with Carl back to KBS.

"You've still got it, kid. You sure you don't want to work full-time with us?" Vincent pressed against the seat back, groaning as he stretched out his muscles.

Carl pointed. "That right there is why I don't want to do this full-time."

"I suppose. I just couldn't sit in an office all day. Working with my hands makes me happy." Vincent held up his hands, calloused, scarred, and sporting a Snoopy bandage on one pinky finger.

"I do too. Just…" Carl used the excuse of waiting for a trio of older women crossing the street to frame his answer.

Having each done time in prison, Vincent and Tomas had overcome obstacles Carl hadn't. Vincent was raised by a single mother, Tomas had a learning disorder, and Carl… Carl had distant, overachieving parents who wouldn't be happy until he occupied a corner office and was making big deals and big decisions. In their eyes, returning to Keeney permanently would be a step down. And while he hated to admit it, a little of that had rubbed off on Carl.

"I like Keeney, there's just more opportunity for me in the capital," he ended lamely.

"Yeah? Like what?"

"Like…" He stared down at the floor mats. "Not having to brush sawdust out of my hair at the end of the day."

Vincent laughed. "There is that."

They were driving through an older neighborhood where new construction butted up against houses that had been there for decades. Carl spotted an older, ranch-style house, similar to his grandmother's, with a For Sale sign in the front yard. He made a mental note to tell Sylvie about it. That made him think about Tomas and his warning. Sylvie would skin her brother alive if she knew about that. Not that he had any intention of telling her because they were friends, coworkers, *and* she'd been hired by his grandmother. Tomas was right, Carl would be leaving soon, so starting something with Sylvie was a bad idea. A bad idea that refused to go away.

CHAPTER 15

Standing fully dressed in a shower with a man was a new experience for Sylvie. Carl heard her giggle and looked down from where he was caulking.

"What?"

"Nothing." She was backed against the molded fiberglass enclosure, applying pressure to close the gap between it and the drywall. Carl stood slightly to her side, arms raised. A bead of sweat trickled down behind his ear, glistening against his skin.

She shut down the image of licking it off. This was Carl, not someone who'd encourage those behaviors. Looking away, she admired the work they'd done on the old bathroom. Widening the doorway and removing the tub had been the biggest job, and Sylvie had subcontracted with KBS for assistance. She and Carl had done the rest.

Sylvie worked alone when she was hired by contractors to mud and tape drywall. So working with someone else was something she hadn't done since she'd finished the Keeney Builds program. She'd expected Carl to challenge her, but he'd been away from hands-on construction long enough that he was happy to leave the decision-making up to her. He did ask questions, though, none of which were annoying. The more time she spent working with Carl, the more time she wanted to spend with him.

"Alright, let's see if that holds." He stepped back and took her hand to pull her away from the shower wall, drawing her so close she could see a tiny scar in his left eyebrow. He smirked down at her. "You're supposed to be checking out the caulking, not me."

She made a face and twisted in the small space, bumping her shoulder against his chest a little harder than necessary. "I'll have to take your word for it. It's too high up for me to—"

Two hands gripped her waist and lifted her.

"Okay, that works." She inspected the smooth, neat line of caulking running around the top of the shower enclosure. There wasn't a gap in sight. "Excellent. We should check on it in an hour or so, but I think it's gonna hold."

Lowering her, Carl stepped out of the shower and made room for her to do the same.

"What's next, boss?" he asked.

"We install the glass wall, the grab bars near the toilet, and then this room is done," she said, moving toward the door.

The slightly rough tile floor was the same throughout the bathroom. Shower doors would have meant a lip for a walker or wheelchair to negotiate, so they planned to install a glass wall to allow easy access and protect the rest of the bathroom from spraying water. A bathing stool would fit easily into the space.

"Great. I'm tired of showering at the gym."

Carl had not complained once about the inconvenience of living through a renovation. With the kitchen totally gutted, he'd set up a folding table in the garage that held a microwave and a hot plate. The refrigerator was there too, and he used the laundry sink to do his dishes.

Sylvie took the cooler full of food from Hola! out to the

deck and set it on the table. She unpacked it as Carl put his phone down and took a seat.

Saying, "I forgot the drinks," he popped up and disappeared into the house.

He'd left his phone screen side up, and when a string of texts came in, Sylvie glanced at it, then picked it up.

Carl returned holding a pitcher and two glasses. "I've been trying to duplicate Gram's iced tea. Tell me what you think."

"I'd prefer you tell me why Dean Sanchez is inviting you to hit balls at the country club," she said coolly.

The smile fell from Carl's face, and he stumbled. Iced tea slopped over the side of the pitcher and spilled onto the ground.

Sylvie set the phone down and pushed it across the table. "You might want to answer. Apparently—and I quote—a chick is there with a rack you won't believe."

She was impressed with her own calm, when inside she wanted to scream, What. The. Fuck!!

The phone dinged again. This time with an image of a woman's cleavage.

"Oh, look. He's sent a picture," Sylvie deadpanned as she settled into a chair.

Carl eyed her warily, like he expected her to throw her food or overturn the table. Anger and hunger were never a good combination, so despite having lost her appetite, she bit into the burrito.

"You're not mad?"

"Oh, I'm mad, but the last time I stormed out in righteous anger, I got evicted. So I'm going to listen to what I hope is a damn good explanation."

"And turn off that stupid phone," she added as the screen lit up with a picture of a woman's golf-skirt-covered behind.

Carl thrust the offending device into his pocket. "I've been dragging my ass trying to figure out how to tell you that my company wants to do business with Sanchez Homes. Them buying our building wrap would be a big contract."

"And a big win for you."

"Yes," he said, meeting her heated gaze directly. "I had lunch with Dean—before I knew who he was—and we hit it off, but it's not going to be an easy sell. Our product is expensive because of our high standards of environmentally sustainable production practices—"

Sylvie held up her hand like a traffic cop. "Spare me the sales pitch and get to the point."

He sighed. "It happened before I knew what he'd done to you."

"Okay. Now that you know that he's a soulless douche canoe, why are you spending time with him?"

"I'm not. He just—" Carl's shoulders slumped and his gaze bounced off her to fix on something in the distance. "—he's stringing me along. He keeps inviting me to do things with him, and when I ask him if his father is on board with buying our product, he changes the subject. And my boss is pushing me."

Finally looking at her, he said, "Trust me. Spending time with Dean Sanchez is the last thing I want to do, but if I don't close this deal, I probably won't get the job in Alaska."

Asshats were everywhere, and she'd sucked it up enough times to appreciate his predicament. Still. "Did you tell your boss what he did to me?"

"No."

She flinched at the bald answer.

"My boss wouldn't't care. It's too big a deal to be sidelined simply because Dean—" he broke off, looking everywhere but at Sylvie.

The joy she'd felt for the last few weeks was snuffed out with that one word: simply. It was good to know that being forced to move and having her money stolen was important only to her. She'd known Carl was ambitious, had admired him for that attribute, but she hadn't known how little he thought of her. Moving slowly and deliberately, she pushed away from the table and stood. Not looking at Carl, she walked through the house, grabbed her bag, and headed for her car.

"Sylvie! Wait!" Carl got between her and the car door, his hands out, placating. "I misspoke. I didn't mean…I'm sorry."

"For what?"

He shook his head but didn't answer, hovering his hands next to her upper arms like he wanted to hold her. She stepped out of his reach.

Unable to meet his eyes for fear he'd see how badly he'd hurt her, she stared at his neck, seeing the pulse beating wildly. Working hard to keep her voice from quavering, she said, "I signed a contract with Miss Jean and I intend to see it through. However, I'd prefer not to work with you. So please find someone else to take your place."

Sidling around him and into her car, she carefully backed out of the driveway and drove off.

*T*he pallet landed slightly off-center on the pile. Carl kicked it into place and went back for another.

"What did that thing do to you?" Ali leaned against the opening in the chain link fence that surrounded warped wood, mis-cut lumber, and broken pallets. Keeney residents were welcome to pick through the lumberyard's discards, but weren't particularly tidy while doing so. Needing somewhere to vent his frustration, Carl had volunteered to clean up the area.

"Nothing."

Ali sipped his coffee and said, "You've been stomping

around for three days, and when you're not doing that, you scowl like a little thundercloud."

"What's going on?" Vincent joined Ali. "Is he in trouble or something?"

"Not that I know of," Ali answered.

Vincent removed his gloves and stuffed them into his back pocket. He leaned against the other side of the opening and crossed his arms. "Does this have anything to do with Sylvie? Hilary said she's been working from home, and she's never done that before."

The mention of Sylvie's name ratcheted up the nausea churning in Carl's gut. It had been there since she'd driven off. Too much of a coward to do the right thing and tell her about Dean, he'd dithered and diminished her. And yet he'd continued to make excuses to Dean and hadn't told his boss about his concerns.

"You look like you're gonna puke," Vincent said. "What's going on?"

Scaling the fence and running away was an option, but Carl doubted he'd get far. He faced the two men. "I screwed up and I…" He had no idea how much they knew about Dean messing with Sylvie and wasn't sure where to start.

"Uh-huh. And?" Ali sipped his coffee. "Come on, kid. Details. I've got shit to do."

"Dean Sanchez screwed over Sylvie," Carl said.

"We know," Vincent replied.

"It's more than him sleeping around and getting her evicted, but that's her story to tell. I'm trying to sell Sanchez Homes on buying my company's building wrap, and I have to go through Dean to do so."

"What does Sylvie think of that?" Ali asked.

"That's the thing. I didn't tell her, and she found out when she saw a text from Dean."

Both men winced.

"How'd she take it?" Ali asked.

"Not good." Carl could still see the look on her face. If he could go back in time, that look would never have been there in the first place. "I said something stupid that made it worse and she told me to find someone to replace me for work on Gram's house and I haven't seen her since then." It was like she'd disappeared off the face of the earth—at least as far as Carl was concerned. Their daily exchange of silly memes and snarky texts had stopped, and he hadn't realized how much he looked forward to them until they were gone.

"Relationships are hard, dude. Suck it up and talk to her," Vincent said.

Carl shook his head. "We're not in a relationship. We just…work together."

Vincent and Ali shared a look, but neither replied.

Ali pushed away from the fence and twisted to look at the loading dock where someone had called his name. He waved, then turned back to Carl. " It took me twenty years to figure out things with Marcia, so I can't help with Sylvie. But I can help you with work. Come talk to me when you're done here."

Carl watched Ali return to the loading dock. "What's that all about?"

Vincent clapped him on the shoulder. "I think he's going to offer you a job."

"He already has, but I'm leaving for Alaska soon."

"Doesn't that depend on you landing the Sanchez Homes contract?"

Carl shrugged one shoulder. "Yeah. What about it?"

"I don't know. Maybe because to get the contract, you have to deal with a self-centered asshat who screwed over someone you care about. And how does that feel?"

"Like shit."

"Then why are you doing it?"

. . .

*V*incent's parting words rang in Carl's head as he trudged up the stairs to the KBS offices. Why was he doing it? Because he didn't have a choice was the immediate answer. Or did he? Deep down, he knew that he did. It would mean less money and less prestige. And less need to chug Maalox on a daily basis.

Feminine laughter floated to him as he reached the top of the stairs, and he quickstepped to the office to find Hilary, Marcia, Fiona, and Iris gathered around the conference table. Sylvie was nowhere in sight. Her desk was tidy, her chair pushed in. There was no evidence that she'd been there that day, and the lightness that carried him into the room drifted away.

"Hey Carl, what's up?" Hilary gestured toward Marcia. "We were just discussing the wedding. Do you have an opinion on morning coats?"

"Not really. Should I?"

The women laughed, and Hilary said, "Ali's waiting for you in his office."

"Thanks," he said, backing out of the room and noting the big smiles on all their faces.

The last room on the upper floor had the name, Ali Haddid, Operations Director, on the door.

Carl knocked on the open door and entered when Ali waved him inside, gesturing at a chair in front of his desk while he spoke on the phone.

Ali had taken over what was originally Iris's office when she did the bookkeeping for KBS. Like the other rooms on the upper level, its window offered a bird's-eye view of the store. One wall was a giant corkboard covered in work schedules, calendars, awards, and invoices, with some photographs thrown in for good measure.

Carl found a photo of himself with Vincent and Tomas, arms akimbo and standing in front of a completed tiny house. There was one from Vincent and Hilary's wedding, one from Tomas and Fiona's wedding, and photos from many other weddings. Carl assumed they were all KBS employees and thought it was nice that Ali would go to all of them.

To Carl's knowledge, his boss at Build Clean didn't attend non-work functions. At least, Carl had never seen him there. Taking a seat, he watched Ali idly trace a finger around a framed photograph of Marcia and him. The smile on Ali's face said it all, and Carl wanted to tease him about it. Instead, he turned away, letting the older man have his private moment. His gaze landed on a bright pink sticky note, and a pang of loss went through him. He'd seen enough of the notes to know this one came from Sylvie.

When he returned to Gram's house at the end of the day, he'd find notes from Sylvie detailing the work that had been accomplished and what was next. It was the only way she communicated with him. He, in turn, would text a response. But they would go unanswered until the next day, when he'd find another sticky note.

"Sorry about that," Ali said, hanging up the phone.

"Not a problem," Carl replied. "So, congratulations on getting engaged. But I gotta know, what took you so long?"

"The truth?" Ali lowered his voice like he didn't want anyone to hear him. "I've put it off because Marcia scares me."

Carl laughed. "I can see that."

"But then she went on a date with the bingo caller at the senior center." He shook his head in disgust. "And I realized that living without her in my life scares me more."

Carl nodded, not knowing what else to say, and then cleared his throat. "You wanted to see me?"

"Ron Sanchez is a good man and runs a good company," Ali said.

"Okay."

"But he has a blind spot when it comes to Dean. He can't see his son for the worthless piece of shit he is. What's the big deal with the Alaska thing?"

"You're gonna give me whiplash if you keep changing the subject," Carl grumbled.

"Good," Ali smirked. "But seriously. Why do you want to move to the frozen tundra?"

"It's a good opportunity."

Ali raised an eyebrow.

The answer sounded lame to Carl's ears as well.

His parents were engineers in the oil and gas industry. They were troubleshooters hired by companies to maximize production and minimize environmental impact. Their company was in its infancy when Carl was born, and for years, Monica and Danny Ryder alternated who stayed home with Carl and his sister, Mandy, while the other worked in the field for whatever company had hired them. When Carl hit middle school and balked at spending summer vacations in isolated work camps in Northern Alberta or the Middle East, he and Mandy moved in with Gram. She was just as strict as her daughter, Monica, regarding completing home-work and doing chores, but she was present, giving her grandchildren her undivided attention.

The new arrangement allowed Monica and Danny to be at the job site simultaneously, and their company flourished. A contract generally lasted only two years, and they worked all over the world, being in high demand. Having been raised with this model, Carl believed that each job led to something bigger. He'd been at Build Clean for more than two years, and the Alaska job would look great on his resume when he was ready to move on to wherever that might be.

Ali, on the other hand, had been with KBS since the early days, when Iris and her husband, Darryl, ran the store. After more than thirty years, he seemed content with where he was and what he did. It wasn't Carl's idea of success.

Or, at least the idea of success that his parents had instilled in him. There was no way to put that into words without sounding like a pompous ass. "Success with the Alaska project will open more doors for me."

"At Build Clean?" Ali continued rocking in his chair, sipping his coffee.

"Yeah. Or, you know, maybe a bigger company."

"So it's a stepping stone."

"Exactly." It was a relief to know Ali understood the game plan.

"And what's at the top?"

"Not quite sure yet. Running a division, probably."

"Will you join your parents' company?"

Carl snorted. "Definitely not. Troubleshooting in the oil patch is their thing, not mine. I enjoy working with people and connecting construction companies with more sustainable practices and products. So the Alaska job would show Build Clean what I can do and move me further up the ladder."

"Do you like moving around?"

The phone rang before Carl could respond, and Ali shot him an apologetic look while taking the call. He listened for a bit, then said, "That works just fine." His eyes on Carl, he added, "I'll take care of that and leave it on your desk for you to finish this evening. Thanks, Sylvie, good job. Bye." He hung up the phone, settled back in his chair, and started rocking again.

"So, do you?"

"What?" Carl had been thinking about Sylvie, wondering where she was and what she was doing.

"Like moving around," Ali said.

"Umm, no. Not really," he replied absently.

"But if Build Clean sends you to another city or state, you'd go?"

"Well, yeah. If that's where the job takes me."

Ali nodded. "What is it about Build Clean that you like?"

"Their commitment to sustainable building practices. There's less waste during production, and when installed properly, their products are more weather-resistant and last longer than those of others. They recognize that construction and building materials themselves need to shift to adapt to climate changes." Carl believed in Build Clean and took pride in working for them.

"And the people you work with?"

"They're great."

"Including your boss?"

"Yep," Carl replied, popping the P.

Ali sipped his coffee and said, "Correct me if I'm wrong, but you're on an unpaid leave of absence, yet they want you to secure a contract with Sanchez Homes. And if you don't, you're out of the running for the Alaska job."

"Yeah."

"So you're working, but not getting paid?"

"It was just a lunch with Dean." He wouldn't mention the phone calls from his boss asking about updates. And emails from coworkers asking about other things.

Ali raised a disbelieving eyebrow.

"What are you getting at?"

Putting his coffee cup down, Ali crossed his arms. "Marcia and I are getting married, and she's going to leave KBS."

"She's retiring?"

"Yep." Ali popped the P. "And I'm offering that job to you."

Slack-jawed, Carl could only stare at him.

"KBS has close ties to the college, Keeney Works, and Keeney Builds. As marketing director, you would strengthen those ties and explore other businesses and community groups with which we can align. Iris doesn't want to expand the business, but she does want to enhance KBS's impact on the community."

"That's…that's…me? You want me for the job?" Both honored and surprised, Carl's voice rose an octave. It was nothing he'd ever thought about.

"Why don't you think you can do it?" Uncrossing his arms, Ali ticked things off on his fingers. "You attended Keeney College and interned here. You've worked here as a general contractor and taught Keeney Builds students. That gives you a solid understanding of KBS. Your time in Olympia with Build Clean has given you insight into the production side. Knowing how materials are made and how those processes are changing can help KBS determine which products to stock. Our customers range from large builders like Sanchez Homes to weekend do-it-yourselfers. Keeping them satisfied keeps them shopping here. So, yeah. You."

"That's a lot."

"It is. And I'll give you some time to think about it. Marcia can tell you what she's currently doing, and Hilary can tell you what she's envisioning."

Ali rose from his chair and headed for the door. Carl followed behind, his head still reeling from their conversation.

He laughed weakly. "I thought you were going to offer me a full-time contracting job."

"I was. But Sylvie suggested the marketing job." He winked and went into the other office, leaving Carl staring after him with his mouth hanging open.

CHAPTER 16

The upside to working from home was that she didn't have to put on hard pants. Truly, she didn't have to put on pants at all. Though she did anyway.

The downside was that Sylvie missed the casual interactions of being at KBS. Ali's dumb jokes, Marcia's big laugh, and the energy and ideas that flowed out of Hilary like water from a faucet. The store was busy in the evening, but the office on the second floor was quiet, and usually, no one was there when Sylvie stopped by.

Her gaze flicked upward as she entered the front doors. Ali's office and the break room were dark, but there was light and movement in the big office. It was probably Hilary. Despite being stupidly happy with Vincent, she was always working. Sylvie quickened her step. Even though she'd asked to work from home, a face-to-face conversation would be nice.

The low hum of conversation greeted her as she rounded the top of the stairs, but it was a man's voice. Carl's voice.

Crap.

Why? Other than to twist the knife he'd stabbed into her heart, he didn't have a reason to be here.

She'd spent the last few days reviewing all their interactions: the text exchanges, meals together, and conversations, and realized she'd read too much into him buying her ice cream or letting her cry on his shoulder. It was a friendship. Period. Not even that, considering he'd been hanging out with Dean despite knowing the damage he'd inflicted on Sylvie. It was clear that Carl didn't care about her, so she needed to package up her tender little feelings and ship them off.

She put on her professional face and entered the office to see Carl sitting at the conference table, staring at his phone. Catching her eye, his smile was small and tentative as he listened to a man on the other side of a video call. His leg bounced under the table. Good, he was nervous too.

Sylvie stood at her desk to review the papers Ali left for her, listening in on the conversation.

"Scott, I don't believe it's in our best interest to continue with this approach. I suggest going directly to the head of Sanchez Homes and bypassing Dean completely." Sylvie looked up to find Carl's eyes on her. "Dean is unscrupulous and unreliable and has a record of screwing people over."

"What has the company done?"

"Not the company, Dean himself. His personal affairs."

"Was it illegal?"

"No. Definitely unethical though." Carl looked unhappy as the other guy sighed heavily.

"Okay. I'll give our legal team a heads-up. In the meantime, I want you to close this deal."

Carl straightened in his chair. "About that. You're going to have to send someone else. I won't work with Dean Sanchez, and I should have told you that a while ago. Furthermore, I am currently on an unpaid leave of absence. I met with Dean as a favor, and now someone else can take over. I'll be back to work in a few weeks."

Scott let out an annoyed sigh and warned, "You're jeopardizing your position here. Don't you want the Alaska job?"

"Yes. But you're taking advantage of me," Carl returned. "I'm pretty sure HR will have something to say about this."

After a brief silence, Scott said, "I think we're done."

Carl tossed his phone on the table and slumped in his chair, rubbing a hand over his jaw.

Sylvie edged over and peeked at the blank screen. "He hung up on you?"

"Yeah."

"What a douche."

Carl snorted. "Yeah."

Everything about him indicated that he hadn't slept in days: his ashy skin, scruffy beard, the lines bracketing his unsmiling mouth, and the bags beneath his eyes. A tiny part of Sylvie was glad. A bigger part of her was worried.

She perched on the edge of a chair. "Can he really fire you?"

"I don't think so. I checked with HR about the parameters of my leave—which I should have done ages ago—and I can't be fired. But that doesn't mean Scott won't hold this over me."

"I'm sorry."

He gave her a sharp look. "You have nothing to be sorry for. I should have told Scott about Dean weeks ago. I should have told *you* about Build Clean and Sanchez Homes as well. Not doing so screwed things up between us, and for that, I am sorry. You deserve better."

"I do?"

"You do," he stated emphatically.

"Why wait until tonight to call him? And why do it here?"

"Because it took a long time to get my head out of my ass and because I knew you'd be here and wanted you to hear it in person. I wasn't sure if you'd believe me otherwise."

"Good call," she replied, sinking back in her chair.

Carl twisted around until his knees were almost touching hers. Leaning close, he said, "I'm really sorry. Can you forgive me?"

The knuckles of his clasped hands had gone white, and she reached out to untangle them, settling her palms into his. "Yes."

Closing his hands around hers, Carl closed his eyes and sighed. "Thank Christ."

"What would you have done if I didn't come in tonight?"

He peeled open one eye and stared at her. "I didn't have a backup plan. Why do you think I was so worried?"

Laughing, she tugged on her hands only for him to tug back and press his forehead against hers. "Thanks, Sylvie," he murmured.

It was hard to speak around the lump in her throat, but she managed to croak, "You're welcome." She was all but surrounded by him and felt the sincerity of his apology through each point of contact: their knees, their hands, their foreheads. Their breath mingled, and she absorbed his relief while he took in her sadness. It was tempting to touch his lips with her own, to find out what he tasted like, to open up and invite him in. But he'd be gone in a few weeks. He'd said so himself, so kissing him was a bad idea.

Squeezing his hands one more time, she reluctantly pulled back and returned to her desk.

After a hectic few days, it was time for the reveal, and she was an absolute wreck. Miss Jean would inspect her house and hopefully be thrilled with the work that had been done. If she wasn't, anything that needed to be redone, be it replacing the paint color or drawer pulls, would come from Sylvie's check. Now that she thought about it, it was a stupid clause to put in the contract. Pure cockiness on her part. However, it was done. The only thing left was to pray to the gods of construction.

Through the large front window, she watched as two vehicles stopped in front of the house. Carl and his grandmother were in one, while the other was a van emblazoned with the Cascades Lodge logo. The side door opened, and a ramp descended, revealing four older women, two of whom were in wheelchairs. Her sister Cara assisted the women out of the vehicle, and the group stood in the driveway, pointing at the house and talking. Sylvie dashed out the back door, across the patio, and down the driveway to greet them.

"Hi," she said, bouncing on her toes and smiling so big her face hurt.

Miss Jean leaned heavily on her walker and murmured a greeting while she stared at the house. Carl's eyes were big as he sidled over to Sylvie.

"Is everything okay?" Sylvie whispered.

"Gram didn't sleep well and is kind of cranky," he whispered back.

"It's not polite to whisper, and I'm not cranky," Miss Jean snapped. "Let's go inside. It's too hot to stand around outside," she said, pushing past Sylvie to the ramp that led to the front door. Carl rolled his eyes at Sylvie and followed his grandmother.

"She's really excited," Cara said, crossing her arms and nudging Sylvie's shoulder as they watched the procession of chattering women.

"It doesn't seem that way," Sylvie grumbled.

"She's been talking about this for days, showing pictures to anyone who'd listen. Then someone told her that she wouldn't make her money back, and she was foolish to spend it on a house she wasn't going to live in. That led to an argument, and now Miss Jean is second-guessing herself."

The clause in the contract regarding changes loomed in Sylvie's mind, and she stared at Miss Jean's back, praying once again that she'd be happy.

The house was no longer a faded cream color with brown trim. It now sported buttery yellow paint with dark green trim. The front door and garage door were painted a lighter green that Sylvie thought really popped. The black metal railing on the wide ramp contrasted nicely, and the new, covered front porch had more than enough room for the group of people gathered there.

"Isn't that the cat's pajamas?" Someone laughed, and the others joined in.

Miss Jean was peering into a facial recognition screen mounted beside the door.

"See, Gram," Carl explained. "It doesn't require a key and locks as soon as the door closes behind you. And the doorbell can be adjusted for people who are hearing impaired. A light will flash inside the house that alerts them when someone rings the bell."

"That is something," she exclaimed, smiling for the first time.

Breathing a sigh of relief, Sylvie said, "I'm going around back to watch them enter. Come with?"

Cara nodded and followed her to the back door. "Ooh, I like this," she said, tapping a toe against the low rubber threshold of the open French doors. They swung open completely to rest against the exterior walls, allowing better mobility. "Well done."

"It's so roomy," a woman in an electric wheelchair said.

"That's because they took out the wall that separated the front room from the kitchen," Miss Jean replied.

What had been a narrow galley kitchen was now a long L-shaped counter above drawers instead of cupboards. The upper cupboards had been replaced with open, reachable shelving. The fridge anchored the shorter end of the L, and a big window opened into a pass-through to the back deck. Where the old Formica table and chairs once stood was a large table with banquette seating on two sides and open space on the other sides for walkers and wheelchairs.

Miss Jean parked herself at one end of the table and preened while her friends oohed and ahhed as they roamed the house.

A loud gasp sounded, and Cara looked at Sylvie, eyebrows raised inquiringly.

"They're checking out the shower," Sylvie explained. "You need to see it too."

Her sister walked away to do so, leaving Sylvie with Carl and Miss Jean.

"What do you think?" Sylvie asked, holding her breath.

Miss Jean held her hands out for Carl and Sylvie to take, and she drew them closer. "Thank you," she said. "You've done a marvelous job, and I am very impressed. I can't believe this is the first time you've done this."

"I can't believe it either," Sylvie replied. With all the help she'd received from Carl and KBS contractors, it had gone much smoother than she'd expected. There had been some minor hiccups, such as the drywall contractor who tried to explain mudding and taping to Sylvie, and the plumber who moonlighted as an Elvis impersonator. Sylvie had had to listen to him sing—off-key—the whole time he'd been there. Resolving her issues with Carl went a long way toward the success of the remodel. That had kept her awake more than worrying about the renovations.

Miss Jean dug through her purse and presented an envelope to Sylvie. "Well, dear, you deserve every penny of this."

Sylvie took the envelope, not knowing what to do with it.

"Go ahead and open it," Miss Jean urged her.

Opening the envelope, Sylvie peeked at the check and gasped. "That's—that's too much."

Carl and Miss Jean exchanged smiles.

"No, it isn't," Carl said. "Gram and I discussed it and believe the amount reflects the quality of your work."

Miss Jean nodded emphatically and stood. "Exactly. Now, Carl, would you please get the food? I think it's time to gloat appropriately." She pushed her walker out to the back deck as Sylvie turned to Carl for an explanation.

"She intends to soak up her friends' congratulations for how smart she was for making this house accessible," he said.

"She won't know that until the house sells, though."

Carl grinned. "She's already received three offers."

"But it hasn't gone on the market yet!"

His grin widened. "I know."

*L*unch on the back deck was a success, and Gram was exceptionally pleased. Toasts were raised to Gram, Sylvie, Carl, KBS, and Sylvie again. He, Sylvie, and Cara abstained, but the others downed two bottles of Sparkling Okanagan Porchbanger Wine and giggled while boarding the van. Gram rode shotgun and Cara drove as the women sang "The Wheels On The Bus" on their return to Cascades Lodge.

Carl and Sylvie cleaned up the lunch remains, did a walk-through of the house for any items left behind, and stood on the lawn.

"What are you going to do now?" he asked.

"Collapse," she said, wobbling her knees like it was imminent.

"The Energizer Bunny needs a recharge," he replied, taking in her drooping demeanor.

He'd heard that during their detente, Sylvie had worked on Gram's house long after the other workers had gone home. Today, Carl discovered touches that weren't in the plans and didn't show up on the invoice: handles instead of doorknobs, angled mirrors in the bathroom and bedroom for people in wheelchairs, a sturdy bench in the shower, and recessed, motion-activated lighting in the hallway floor. He wished he'd been there to assist. There was so much he needed to make up to her.

"Agreed," she said, rolling her shoulders and cranking her neck from side to side.

He stepped behind her, cupped her shoulders, and pressed his thumbs into the rigid tendons on the back of her neck. "I have an idea." She groaned, and he increased the pressure. "How about you go home and take a nap, I'll zone out in front of the baseball game, then I'll come get you and take you out to dinner."

"Dinner?" she squeaked. "You want to take me out to dinner?"

"Yes." He continued stroking his thumbs up the back of her neck, inhaling the fragrance of her shampoo. Little curls had escaped her customary ponytail, and on an impulse, he pulled out the hair tie and started massaging her scalp. The groan that came out of her hit him low and hard.

"You keep that up and I'm going to start drooling," she said, slowly pulling away. When she turned around, her dark hair hung in heavy waves over her shoulders, and it was a different Sylvie he was looking at, with pink cheeks and heavy-lidded eyes. He thought he'd seen that look once before, when she'd accepted his apology in the KBS conference room. He'd wanted so badly to kiss her then and had cursed himself all the way home for being a coward. But no more. The renovation was complete, removing a barrier that had been blocking them from moving forward.

He flexed his hands, wanting to bury them in her hair again, draw her closer, see if she tasted as good as she looked. A poke in the chest brought him back to the present.

"What time should I expect you?"

They agreed on a time, and he watched her drive off before going back inside. He sprawled on the couch, but instead of watching the game, he fell asleep, dreaming of Sylvie, her hair hanging over bare shoulders, his hands roaming over her inviting frame.

CHAPTER 17

Hours later, he parked his truck between Sylvie's dusty Subaru and a bright yellow Mini in Iris's driveway. The garage door was open, and he saw Iris talking to Ingrid, who, he'd heard recently, had moved into the tiny house in Iris's backyard. The women smiled as he approached and greeted them.

"Don't you look nice," Iris said, brushing a hand across his shoulder.

"Thanks," he replied, not wanting to tell them that he'd gone out and bought a new shirt because all of his shirts bore either the Build Clean or KBS logo.

"You might want to remove the tag, though," Ingrid said.

He did so and turned at the sound of footsteps.

Sylvie stood at the top of the stairs, stuffing something into a tiny purse. She'd done something with her hair, and it fell in soft waves that framed her face and fell about her shoulders. She wore a simple, soft peachy sundress that looked anything but simple on her. It highlighted smooth tan skin that glowed in the evening sun, hinted at cleavage, and skimmed her hips before stopping just above her knees. He'd seen her in jeans and overalls and leggings and shorts. But never in a dress and never in heels.

His gaze fixed upon her, Carl drifted toward the staircase. And not a moment too soon.

Sylvie caught a heel on one step and pitched forward.

Carl's steps turned to strides, and he grabbed her two steps from the bottom. Hands clasped around her waist, he stared up at her. "I've got you. Did you hurt anything?"

"Just my dignity." Sylvie laughed shakily. She gripped the railings and tilted her head at her feet. "There's a reason I don't wear heels. Clumsy is my middle name."

Carl thought "stunning" was her middle name, but he simply smiled, releasing his grip and stepping back.

"Where are you going?" Iris asked, her smiling gaze ping ponging between Carl and Sylvie.

"Where *are* we going?" Sylvie asked. She'd put on makeup, too. Something that made her eyes look bigger and brighter, and her lips shine.

"Hmm?"

She repeated the question.

He blinked. "Denali's. Is that okay?" The restaurant complex was a Keeney favorite, offering great food, but was it too casual?

"That's perfect."

He hurried to open the passenger door of the truck, thankful that he'd cleaned it recently. Sylvie smiled her thanks and climbed in, giving him a flash of smooth thigh. He was practically sweating by the time he slid behind the wheel.

Luck was on his side, and he quickly found a spot in the crowded parking lot. Sylvie was out of the truck before he had a chance to help her, and now he didn't have an excuse to take her hand. He moved to her side, and they walked to the old elementary school that had been converted into a hotel, with four restaurants surrounding a large patio. Their reservation was in one of the smaller restaurants, and they were led to a table by a smiling hostess.

The server who brought them water and took their drink order knew Sylvie, and they talked about people they had in common.

"Do you know everyone in Keeney?" Carl asked as the woman left them.

"Sometimes it feels that way," Sylvie replied. "Sometimes I wish I could be anonymous, like when I go into the drugstore to buy medication for a yeast infection, but for the most part I like having people around me who care enough to ask about me and my family."

Carl nodded solemnly and looked at her intently. "How are you? And how is your family?"

Her laughter rang out, making him grin.

"My family is fine," she said. "And I am great now that the house is done and your grandmother approves of everything."

"She does." Carl lifted his glass in a toast. "We were originally going to spackle any holes, slap on some paint, then put it on the market. With the accessibility renovations you made, the house is 1000 times better. Gram is sifting through the offers, and I expect it will be sold in the next few weeks."

"That will be a big weight off your shoulders."

Carl blew out an exaggerated sigh. "It will indeed."

"Are you going to—"

"Well now, don't you two look cozy." Dean loomed over their table. His glittering gaze slid over Sylvie. "I always did like that dress on you. I have fond memories of taking it off you."

Before Carl could respond, Sylvie cocked her head to the side and laughed like his inappropriate comment was water off a duck's back. "Really? I remember you not being able to get it up and then passing out. This dress deserved better than that."

Dean's smirk turned into a scowl. Turning his back on Sylvie, he said to Carl, "You ignored my calls, and Build Clean contacted Dad. What gives?"

Standing, Carl smelled the alcohol fumes wafting off Dean. "I'm on a leave of absence, and someone else from Build Clean will be the contact point."

"Yeah, no. I don't buy it. She had something to do with it." Dean pointed at Sylvie. "You're trying to make me look bad."

"You're managing to do that all by yourself." Sylvie gestured to the people staring at Dean.

"This isn't over," he snapped and stalked off.

Carl sank into his chair and reached for Sylvie's clenched hand. "You okay? I am so sorry for that."

"It's fine," Sylvie said, looking anything but fine. "I was bound to run into him sooner or later. I just hope I haven't screwed things up for you."

"What? No! I got an email from my boss at Build Clean. They'll leave me alone until my leave is up and I'm still in the running for the Alaska job. It's all good."

Their drinks arrived, and Sylvie sipped her wine, still looking shaken.

"Are you sure you're okay? We can go somewhere else."

She shook her head. "Seriously, I'm fine. But I do need to use the restroom."

"Okay." Carl stood as she rose from the table and walked off, head high and back stiff.

The evening had lost its glow before it even started.

Sylvie bypassed the restrooms and ducked around the building to a quiet, dark corner. Closing her eyes, she slumped against the rough, brick wall and took a deep breath. She'd showered and shaved and primped and fussed, all for naught. When she suggested to Ali that he offer the marketing job to Carl, he liked the idea. But she hadn't heard a word since then. Carl must have turned it down. Apparently, his heart was set on moving to Alaska. Whatever was between them—and there was definitely something there—would not last beyond a couple of weeks. So why bother?

Then she remembered the smoldering look in his eyes this afternoon. The feel of his hands when he'd caught her on the stairs. That. *That* was why she'd bothered. Dean had been adequate, but something told her that Carl would be far more than adequate. Determined to have a few good memories to look back on after he'd left, she smoothed her dress over her hips and stepped away from the wall to return to the table.

And bumped into Dean.

"Oops," he said, grasping her biceps.

"Lovely," she grumbled and pulled away.

He blocked her path, saying, "What's your hurry? Going back to the kid? Isn't he a little young for you?"

"I don't know why you insist on being an asshat. Now get out of my way."

"We're not done, Sylvie. You owe me, and I want—" he belched "—an apology."

"Uh-uh. Absofreakinglutely not," she said. "You cheat on me, get me evicted, then empty my bank account. In what universe do I owe you?"

"You made me look bad."

She scoffed, "And how did I do that?"

He jerked his head toward the restaurant. "Pretty boy trash-talked me to Build Clean, and now I'm out of the loop on that deal. Do you know what that's worth?"

"No, Dean, I don't." She was weary of the conversation

and the pouting man-child in front of her. "And here's the thing. Instead of sleeping with me, moving in with me, and sliding into my bank account, if you had asked me to invest in your business, I probably would have said yes."

"Yeah," he smirked, "but I needed a place to crash, and I wouldn't have had a taste of that sweet ass of yours."

God, he was disgusting. How had she not seen that sooner? She'd been taken in by his pretty words and pretty face and was an idiot. She turned on her heel and stalked back to the table, her determination to make the best of her time with Carl now replaced with her determination to get away from Dean.

Carl rose, his welcoming smile turning to alarm. "Are you okay?"

She shook her head. Bitching and moaning about her bad choices wouldn't do either of them any good, and she wasn't going to be very good company tonight. "Not really, would you mind taking me home?"

Nodding, he threw some bills on the table and gestured toward the door.

Staring out the window, she was silent on the drive home, aware of the looks Carl was sending her.

"Are you sure you're alright?" Carl asked when they arrived. He turned off the engine and reached for her hand. He was so sweet, and a chorus of if-onlys ran through her head.

"I will be," she said.

"Is there anything I can do?"

Stay. It was tempting to say the word aloud and invite him in. But he wasn't staying, and his departure was already going to hurt. Spending the night with him would only make it worse. "No thanks," she said and got out of the truck.

"At least let me walk you to the door." He followed her up

the stairs, waited while she unlocked the door, and put a hand on her arm. "If you need anything, let me know. I'm only a phone call away."

His dark eyes were full of concern, and his hand was warm and comforting. Pushing up on her toes to kiss his cheek, she wobbled in her heels and missed the mark, connecting with his mouth instead. Time stopped for a moment, then he slid his hand up her arm to her shoulder and drew her in.

Pulling back was the smart thing to do. Pulling back, saying goodnight, and letting him leave. Sylvie didn't want to be smart. She wouldn't have this opportunity for much longer and wanted to feel. She reached up to cup his neck and pull him closer.

Carl kissed her firmly, like it wasn't an accident, and he knew exactly what he was doing. He licked along the seam of her lips, then kissed his way up her jaw to hum just beneath her ear. She trembled at the vibration and angled her neck, an invitation for him to do more. One hand on her shoulder, he slipped the other up her back and under her hair to hold the back of her head, strumming the cords of her neck until she was putty.

Sylvie wobbled and stared up at him. The porch light wasn't on, and all she could see was the flash of his teeth.

"I should go," he said.

"You don't have to," she replied.

He traced a calloused thumb across the apple of her cheek, and she scratched her nails through his tight curls. His eyes closed and opened to reveal a heated gaze that nearly set her aflame. "You keep that up and I won't."

She giggled then winced.

"What?"

She sighed and pulled back, pointing at her feet. "These shoes are killing me."

He scooped her up and carried her to a patio chair.

Setting her down, he kneeled before her, removed one shoe, and then the other. "Why wear them then?" he asked as she moaned, curling and flexing her toes.

"Because they're cute and they go with the dress."

"Babe," he said, taking one foot and rubbing his thumbs up the instep to the base of her toes.

The word was laced with humor and fondness, and she wanted to hear it again and again. She poked a toe against his ribs, and he scowled but kept rubbing her feet. Closing her eyes, she leaned back, feeling like a wet noodle.

"I'm sorry we ran into Dean," he murmured.

"You couldn't have known."

"Yeah," Carl sighed, "but he ruined our evening."

It would be very easy to let him believe Dean's presence was the reason. But she was tired of the ticking clock and living on tenterhooks. Sylvie pulled her foot out of his hands and sat up. "Not exactly. However, running into him certainly wasn't a highlight."

"Then what was it?" He snagged another chair and sat, close enough that their knees touched.

"You kiss really good."

"O-kay," he drawled. "And that's a problem?"

"It *is* a problem because you're going away."

"Am I?"

"Aren't you taking the job in Alaska?"

She'd clenched her hands over her knees, and Carl placed his on top of them. "Not necessarily. Ali offered me Marcia's job. But you already know that."

She shrugged one shoulder and didn't meet his gaze.

"Thank you for that."

"Are you going to take it?"

"It hit me out of the blue, but I'm giving it some serious consideration."

"What's there to consider?" A bubble of hope had been rising, but it sank back down.

Carl leaned back, lacing his hands behind his head and staring at the night sky. "I had a plan that involved a big company in a big city."

The bubble of hope popped. "I see," she said.

"However," he continued, "I didn't know that I was limiting myself. That small towns and small businesses have big rewards. Like friends, and family, and"—he nudged her knee—"a beautiful woman who makes work boots look sexy."

"Oh," she said, unclenching her hands.

He brought his hands down, widened his legs, and pulled her chair closer until his knees bracketed hers. Tipping her chin up, he brushed his thumb across her bottom lip. "There are things that need to be tied up with Build Clean because I don't want to burn my bridges, but if I stay, will I be able to kiss you on the regular?"

"Possibly," she said, and nipped his thumb.

He growled, and she grinned.

Sylvie leaned closer to press her lips against his. He moved his hands from the chair to her hips and spread his fingers to grip her behind, pulling her closer. Yeah, she'd let him kiss her on the regular. And more.

He deepened the kiss, teasing her tongue, biting her bottom lip, and then soothing it with gentle sucks. She gripped his biceps to prevent herself from collapsing, drowning in his deliciousness. Her stomach growled, and she ignored it, reveling in the feel of his hands moving up and down her thighs. It growled again, and Carl pulled back, quirking an eyebrow at her.

"Ignore it," she said.

"I don't think I should. I asked you to dinner, so let's get you fed. Mind if I check out your fridge?"

It was on the tip of her tongue to say, *You can check out more than my fridge.* Instead, she said, "Not at all."

Carl said as he followed her into the house, "Now, take a seat and prepare to be dazzled by my culinary capabilities."

"You haven't seen the contents of my fridge yet. What if there's nothing you can use?"

He kissed her on the nose. "Then prepare to be dazzled by my ability to order takeout."

Sylvie laughed and settled at the kitchen table to watch him. He poured each of them a glass of wine and set about making omelets. While they ate, Carl told her stories about living with his grandmother, how he was greeted every Saturday morning with a list of chores to do. Her mantra was *if you can read, you can cook,* and he'd learned to make bread and, in his words, "the flakiest damn piecrust you've ever tasted." Sylvie, in turn, told him about working in her mother's restaurant, and they traded stories about miserable experiences in the dish pit.

They were cleaning up the kitchen together as a car pulled into the driveway. Ingrid got out and walked across the yard without looking up. She slipped inside the tiny house and turned on a light.

"When did she move in?" Carl asked.

"Yesterday."

"And that's working out okay?"

"Yeah," Sylvie replied truthfully. "It was not how I pictured making a new friend, but that's what she's become. We're thinking of forming a club for all the people who've been screwed over by Dean."

"I've a feeling you'd need a banquet hall for that."

Laughing, she took Carl's hand and led him to the couch. One arm around her, he drew her down beside him and traced the contours of her face with a finger. His dark eyes were warm, and she felt that he could see to her very soul.

"What are you thinking?" he asked.

"That I'm glad I cleaned the apartment today."

His eyes crinkled, and he pulled back to look around the room. "This is certainly a lot nicer than my place."

"You mean Miss Jean's house?"

He shook his head. "No, my place in Olympia. I've got a couch, a TV, and a bed. There's nothing on the walls except a calendar, and I have the bare minimum in the kitchen."

"How long have you been there?"

He made a face. "Three years."

"Really?" Sylvie had lived in her suite for almost two months, yet it felt like she'd been there forever. The leather couch, matching armchair, and square wooden coffee table had originally belonged to her brother, but the bright pillows, soft throws, and area rug were her own. Framed photographs of her family lined the mantel, and she'd hung framed posters of iconic Washington State landmarks: Mt. Rainier, Pike Place Market, Snoqualmie Falls, and the Skagit Valley tulip fields. They weren't expensive, but they were bright and made her smile.

"Why didn't you spiff the place up?"

He raised an eyebrow at her. "Spiff?"

She stuck out her tongue. "You know what I mean."

He settled into the corner of the couch and was about to prop his socked feet on the coffee table, but stopped. "Do you mind?"

"Nope." Sylvie put her feet on the table, liking the feel and look of Carl lounging beside her.

He relaxed back with one arm around her shoulders, curling his fingers around her bicep. "I never really thought of it as a home, just a place to stay. I didn't expect to be there long, and I spent most of my time at work anyway. I guess I just didn't see the point. The good thing about it is that when I move on, there's very little to pack."

He altered their positions until he lay on the couch with Sylvie pressed up against him. "I think there are better things we can do than discuss my lack of decorating skills," he murmured against her ear. She shivered and turned to press her lips against his.

They made out on the couch until Sylvie's brain was mush and her lips were swollen in the nicest possible way. It wasn't until well after he'd left and she was snuggled in her bed that she realized he hadn't said where his next destination would be. Only that he'd be moving on.

CHAPTER 18

*E*arlier that evening, Ingrid had watched Carl close the truck's door for Sylvie and hustle around into the driver's side.

Beside her, Iris sighed. "They're such a cute couple."

"Yes they are," Ingrid agreed. When the truck was out of sight, she asked her new landlady, "How much will it cost to store my things?" The tiny house had a built-in couch and dining area, so she didn't need what she'd bought when she moved to Keeney.

Iris waved away her question. "Nothing. There's more than enough room in the garage, and it's not in the way."

"Are you sure?" Ingrid did not want to take advantage of her employer. She was grateful to have been offered the tiny house. KBS paid a decent wage, but it wasn't what she'd been earning at the bank, and she could no longer afford the rent on her apartment after the bank had let her go.

She didn't like saying "fired," even though that's what had happened. She'd screwed up and gotten canned. All because of Dean Sanchez. God, she was stupid.

"Absolutely," Iris assured her. "Now, I'm going to the church for game night. You're welcome to come with me."

"Thank you, but no. I still have some unpacking to do. You have a good time."

Iris got in her car and drove off, and Ingrid wandered back to her new place. The tiny house really was lovely and certainly had enough room for her. She put her dishes in the kitchen cupboards, hung up her clothes, and personalized the space by adding toss pillows and an afghan to the couch. And then she was done. It was seven o'clock on a Friday night, and she had nothing to do, so she made a cup of tea and took it, along with a book, outside to sit on the small patio beside her house.

The yard was well-maintained and peaceful, which wasn't surprising considering how much time Iris spent in it. Ingrid's gaze settled on the upper level of the house where Sylvie lived. The woman had a huge heart. She had enough influence at KBS to have gotten Ingrid fired, and considering the circumstances of their first meeting, she wouldn't have blamed Sylvie. Instead, Sylvie had befriended her, even invited her to join the softball team. For the first time since moving to Keeney, Ingrid didn't feel lonely.

Her phone flashed with a text from Dean Sanchez: *I'm at Denali's. Join me.*

A booty call?

She picked up the phone, contemplating telling him to lose her number. She hadn't seen or heard from him since being fired. Her calls and texts went unanswered, and it took her a while to realize just how much she'd been used. His cocky smile and flattering words had warmed her lonely little heart, and she'd scuttled her career as a result.

Her gaze fixed on her Mini parked near Sylvie's Subaru. It wasn't fair that Dean strutted around like the entitled asshole he was while their lives had been uprooted.

Searching for the middle finger emoji, she landed on the thumbs-up emoji and hit Send. Maybe, just maybe, there was a way to get back at him.

Half an hour later, she found Dean at the bar of one of Denali's restaurants. "Hey," she said, settling on the stool beside him.

His bleary-eyed gaze roamed her features before lighting with recognition. "Hey doll, what are you doing here?"

"You called me and I thought it would be nice to catch up." She played with the V-neck of her shirt, drawing his attention to her cleavage. "I've missed you."

"I've missed you, too," he slurred, staring at her chest.

Fighting back a shiver of revulsion, she trailed a hand up his thigh. "Want to get out of here? How about I drive you home?"

"That's the best idea I've had all night," he said, sliding off the stool. He slapped some bills on the bar, slung an arm around Ingrid's shoulder, and they headed to the exit.

Taking him home was easier said than done. He mumbled directions, then fell asleep, and she took a few wrong turns before finding his building. He roused enough to pull out his keys and lead her inside. The place was a pit and smelled worse. Empty takeout containers and beer cans littered the coffee table and kitchen counters, and a mound of dirty laundry occupied a chair.

Ingrid's lip curled, and she didn't bother to hide it. Dean wouldn't have noticed anyway.

"Wanna party?" he asked, plopping heavily on the couch and reaching for a half-smoked joint.

"You start without me," she said. "I have to use the bathroom."

He nodded like a bobblehead and lit up.

Finding the bathroom, she wished she'd brought rubber gloves. The room wasn't any cleaner than the kitchen, and she shuddered, glad she didn't need to pee. Apparently, Dean went through his mail while sitting on the toilet because the top of the tank was stacked with flyers and unpaid bills. Ingrid snapped photos with her phone and put them back.

Tiptoeing into the bedroom across the hall, she closed the door most of the way and risked turning on the light. An explosion of laundry and tangled sheets greeted her.

On their first date, Ingrid had told Dean about her grandmother, who owned rental properties in Wenatchee. She'd shown Ingrid a bookshelf full of ledgers that she used for bookkeeping. Even though her grandmother used a computer, she didn't quite trust cloud storage and took comfort in maintaining paper records. Dean had said that he did something similar because he didn't want prying eyes to access his business.

At the time, Ingrid was mesmerized by his charm and hadn't given much thought to his comment. Now she wondered what exactly he wanted to keep secret. Three banker's boxes in the corner caught her eye, but a noise from the living room had her moving quickly to the door.

She slipped through the crack and retraced her steps. Dean was flat on his back, snoring, the joint still smoldering between his fingers. Heaving a sigh of relief, Ingrid stubbed out the joint and returned to the bedroom.

The first two boxes contained sports memorabilia, but she struck gold on the third, which contained a stack of leather-bound ledgers dating back five years.

She recalled Dean going on about starting up his new business the previous year, but being stalled by a lack of funding. He'd been pissed that his father refused to invest, insisting that Dean make his own way.

Ingrid found entries showing the opening balance and modest deposits being made every four or five weeks in the previous year. Nothing that made her spidey-sense tingle. She put the box away and returned to the living area. Dean was still passed out, one hand shoved down the front of his pants, the other flung across his chest. She shook her head. *How had she found this man attractive?*

The dining room table was the only cleanish area in the

place. It held a laptop, a stack of papers, a leather notebook, and a ledger. She opened the laptop, and the computer came to life, displaying an image of a smirking Dean. *Now, what would be the password?* On a hunch, she carried the laptop over to Dean and angled the screen over his face. It worked.

He may have kept ledgers for money transactions, but his email was unsecured and told a very interesting story. Using her phone, she snapped images of conversations and their corresponding ledger entries.

*W*hat to do now? She'd slipped out of the apartment and taken off like a thief in the night. Was she? Her conscience rose to the surface and nagged at her as she drove around town until she ended up in the Keeney UMC parking lot. Game night was ending, and people were saying their goodnights and taking off.

Voices came from the fellowship hall as she entered the building, but she didn't recognize anyone, so she walked down the wide hallway to the chapel. A light shone on the cross in the window; otherwise, the room was empty. Ingrid sat in a pew, nibbling on her bottom lip. She'd hoped to find Iris. Her landlady might look like a mousy old lady, but she was a savvy businesswoman who'd been buffeted by life. She scrolled through the photographs, evidence of Dean's wrongdoing, her thumb hovering over the delete icon.

She bobbled the phone when the door opened behind her, catching her unaware.

"Sorry about that. I didn't know anyone was here." An Asian man, wearing a clerical collar under a Deadpool T-shirt, smiled at her. "I'm Pastor Andy."

"Hi, I'm Ingrid. You probably want to lock up, so I'll get out of your way."

"That's not necessary," he replied, taking a seat in a pew two rows up from her. "I come in here at the end of the day to let him"—he nodded toward the cross—"know how the day went, and decompress."

He shifted in his seat to grin at her. "That way I don't complain to my husband when I get home."

Tension eased from Ingrid, and she smiled back. After a few minutes of quiet, she said hesitantly, "Do you hear people's confessions? And like, keep it private?"

Pastor Andy twisted around. "Yes and no. People do tell me their problems, and I maintain confidentiality. However, if someone has been harmed as a result of your actions, I will likely report it. Has someone been harmed?"

"Yes," she replied, then hurried on, "but not physically, and not because of *my* actions."

"Ahh. Because of someone else's actions?"

"Yes," she said, holding up her phone, "and I have proof of it."

"And did you obtain that proof legally?"

Ingrid didn't meet his gaze. "I didn't break into his house and take anything. I just…saw something."

"Will someone *be* harmed because of your actions?"

Now that was a good question. "The guy is a smug, self-serving prick, and I doubt it's possible for him to be hurt," she blurted, then uttered a hasty, "Sorry, pastor."

"Not a problem. Let me get this straight. You stumbled—" he put air quotes around the word "—upon evidence of wrongdoing. If you did nothing with it, would that cause harm to someone else?"

"Yes!" The transactions clearly showed Dean siphoning money from Sanchez Homes.

Pastor Andy locked his fingers together, leaning against the pew back. "Do you want to stop the smug, self-serving prick from harming that person, or do you want payback?"

"Both?" She heaved a sigh. "He used me, and because of that, he was able to use someone else. It wasn't illegal, just shitty. Then I stumbled upon evidence that he's stealing from —someone very close to him."

"Will *that* someone benefit from knowing about it? That might sound like a dumb question, but what is the worst that can happen if they don't find out?"

Sanchez Homes was a big company and could sustain the loss for quite a while; however, it wouldn't go unnoticed forever. When it did come to light, Dean's family would be devastated. Ingrid had met his parents through the bank and thought they were lovely people. Hurting them wasn't something she wanted to do, but they deserved to know.

Heaving a sigh, Ingrid rose from the pew. "Thank you for your time, pastor. I think I know what I need to do."

"Glad to hear it. And I hope to see you again. Preferably, when you haven't been honing your cat burgling skills."

She laughed, and blushed, and left the church with a different problem on her hands. How to inform Dean's parents.

CHAPTER 19

Decked out in flowers and tulle, the small chapel at the church looked lovely. Ali stood beside his brother Tal, clenching and unclenching his hands until the music started and Vincent walked his mother down the aisle. Then, Ali's posture relaxed, and he beamed. Stopping in front of Pastor Andy, Vincent kissed his mother's cheek, handed the bouquet to Iris, her attendant, and then joined Marcia's hands with Ali's. When he turned and wiped away a tear, a sigh went up from the wedding guests.

Sylvie sighed right along with them. Wedged between her parents and Cara and Sierra, her gaze bounced between the ceremony and Carl, who sat beside Miss Jean, two pews ahead of her. His dark blue suit gleaming in the sunshine coming through the stained-glass windows, he looked crisp and sharp, totally at ease, and totally mouthwatering.

He'd been over every night since their date at Denali's. They'd eat, play video games, talk, and kiss. Lots and lots of kissing, but never more than that. As much as he participated enthusiastically, often initiating, he seemed to hold back, and Sylvie didn't know what to do. If an erection served as proof, she knew he was as aroused as she was, so why would he leave just as they were getting to the good part?

An elbow to her ribs and a sharp glance from her mother drew Sylvie's attention back to the ceremony, and she clapped along with everyone else as Marcia threw her arms around Ali and planted an enthusiastic kiss on him.

KBS had closed its doors for the day due to the fact that every employee was invited to the wedding. From the crowded pews, Sylvie was pretty sure they'd all shown up. There were many she didn't recognize because she'd never seen them in anything but workwear. Her gaze was drawn back to Carl. In her opinion, he outshone everyone in attendance, even the bride.

Hours later, the deejay played a slow song, and couples moved closer on the small dance floor. Someone had dimmed the lights, making the space more intimate. Cara and Sierra swayed next to Sylvie's parents, and Hilary giggled at something Vincent said.

She looked around for Tomas and Fiona, surprised they weren't on the dance floor. She spotted them sitting at a table, where Fiona had removed her shoes and was sitting with her head back, rubbing her baby bump while Tomas rubbed her feet. Marcia and Ali weren't dancing either. They were at another table filled with laughing people, Ali's arm draped possessively around Marcia's shoulders.

Sylvie had been to many wedding receptions in the banquet room of her mother's restaurant, but she thought this one topped them all. Not because it was overly decorated, but because the atmosphere was so joyous. She'd eaten her fill, talked and laughed with the people at her table, and had even danced a few times. But not with Carl. In fact, she'd barely spoken to him as he'd sat at another table and then taken his grandmother home. She looked down at her phone to see if he'd texted when she felt a presence behind her. She looked up, and he was there. "Dance with me?" he asked, holding out a hand.

He swallowed, and she watched the movement of his throat in fascination. "Sure."

The opening bars of "Tennessee Whiskey" started up as she rose from the table to join him. She stepped into his arms on the dance floor, one hand on his shoulder, the other clasped loosely against his chest. They swayed in silence, and she was aware of his hand stroking up her back, his thumb brushing against the bare skin of her shoulder blades. He'd removed his jacket and in slim-fitting trousers and an unbuttoned dress shirt, he looked tasty. A bead of sweat had trickled down his throat, and she wanted to lick it off. Drawing closer, she smelled his cologne. A spicy scent he'd never worn before but suited him perfectly.

Feeling better now that she was in his arms, she asked the question that had been on her mind for days, "Before you moved away, how come you never asked me out? It might have been me, but I thought we'd had a connection."

"Oh, no. We definitely had a connection," Carl said, widening his eyes dramatically, "but your brother would have killed me."

"What?"

His firm grip was the only thing that prevented her from stumbling. "When you went through Keeney Builds and then started working at KBS, I asked him if you were dating anyone, and he told me you were off limits."

"Really?"

"I didn't push it because I knew that I was leaving. Should I have?"

"Maybe?" They'd been friends and she'd enjoyed his company at the time. What would have happened if they had dated? Could they have made it work? "Hang on for a moment."

She stalked over to her brother and whacked him on the arm.

"Ow! What's that for?" Tomas scowled up at her.

"For being an interfering moron."

Fiona's laughter rang out as Sylvie returned to Carl.

"Everything okay?" Carl asked, taking her in his arms again.

"Much," she replied, narrowing her eyes at Tomas behind Carl's back.

They lapsed into a comfortable silence listening to the song, and Carl's hand made its way to the small of her back, and he drew her closer to him.

"You smell good," he said, his voice a low rumble that sent shivers down her spine.

"I normally smell like spackling compound."

"No you don't," he replied. "You always smell like sunshine in springtime."

She looked up at him. "Does sunshine even have a smell?"

"Sure it does," he pressed his nose against the top of her head. "It smells like you. Fresh and full of promise."

Tempted to roll her eyes and tell him his pick-up lines needed work, there was so much sincerity in his eyes, she bit her tongue and squeezed his hand.

A burst of laughter drew their attention to a packed table.

"What do you think that's all about?" Carl asked.

With Ali sitting on one side of her, Marcia leaned against Iris, both convulsing with laughter. Ali's brother Tal sat next to Iris, grinning broadly. Sylvie's parents were also at the table, her father shaking his head while her mother giggled.

The song ended, and Sylvie took Carl's hand. "Let's find out."

They joined Vincent, Hilary, Tomas, and Fiona, who'd also been drawn by the hilarity.

"What's going on?" Sylvie asked.

Vincent grinned. "Apparently, those two—" he pointed at Iris and Marcia "—are the masterminds behind one of Keeney's most mysterious pranks."

"You know how people set out lawn chairs days before the 4th of July parade?" Sylvie and Carl nodded. No one knew when the tradition started, but the sidewalks surrounding the intersection of Main Street and Keeney Avenue would be clogged with lawn chairs. "One New Year's Eve about ten years ago—they're arguing about when, exactly—Iris and Darryl, Marcia and Ali, and two other couples, chained lawn chairs to the bench in front of the bank with a laminated sign that said 'Reserved for July 4th Parade. Do not move.'"

"I remember that," Carl said. "It made the newspaper, and Gram showed me the photo. I thought it was funny."

"It gets better," Vincent replied, pointing at Iris. "Our boss, one of Keeney's most esteemed business leaders, sent a letter to the editor complaining about the entitlement of some people and implying that the city was charging reservation fees for the best spots on the parade route. The letter gained traction on the community's Facebook page, and people were up in arms. It even made it onto the evening news, and Iris was one of the people interviewed."

"Apparently," Vincent made air quotes, "she just happened to walk by when the camera crew was set up outside the bank. When they asked her opinion, she said that the spot in front of the bank was the best viewing location for the parade and she wished she'd thought of it."

Everyone looked at Iris with new eyes. In a lavender dress, pearls, and her gray hair styled in a chignon, she looked as innocent as a lamb.

"So, what happened to the chairs?" Hilary asked.

Marcia looked up and grinned. "People left them alone. They might have complained, but no one touched them."

"Although," Ali added, "each month, a laminated sign

would appear that advertised a local business. For Valentine's Day, the ad was for Keeney Cards & Sweets. March was for Pint Night at an Irish Pub."

"And you did that?" Tal asked, sending Iris a look of admiration.

She blushed and demurred, "I only did the first two. Marcia did the others."

Marcia shook her head. "It wasn't me. Maybe Darryl?"

Iris scoffed. "Darryl thought we were being foolish. The only reason he agreed to the stunt in the first place was because you wouldn't stop nagging him."

"Me?" Marcia splayed a hand over her chest. "I've never nagged anyone in my life." When half the room erupted in laughter, she relented. "Maybe I nag once in a while."

Ali pulled her in for a kiss. "You can nag me for the rest of our lives."

Marcia smiled up at him like he'd hung the moon.

"How did you get away with it?" Fiona asked. "There are security cameras all over downtown Keeney."

"There weren't at that time," Marcia answered. "We chose the bank because there weren't any restaurants close by, and we did it at midnight because everyone was down at the park for the fireworks. Our old neighbors acted as lookouts and provided a diversion."

Iris started giggling uncontrollably again. Sylvie nudged Carl. It was fun seeing their boss enjoying herself so much.

"You have to understand," Marcia explained, "Joyce used to be in theatre, and she insisted everyone be in costume. Darryl, the party pooper, refused, but Joyce told him that his role was that of a guy out for an evening walk, and he could wear his own clothes. We all," she gestured at Iris and Ali, "did the same. Nick and Mac were the diversion. Joyce made them wear ugly Christmas sweaters while they played badminton in the next intersection."

Vincent gaped. "You mean Nick? The guy who used a

ruler to measure the length of his grass did something so… juvenile?"

Iris bobbed her head. "The one and the same."

"I'll be damned." Vincent turned to Hilary. "I don't think I ever saw that guy smile the whole time he lived next door. I guess still waters do run deep."

Iris nudged Marcia. "Tell them what Joyce and Lorna did."

"They really got into it. They were both decked out like cat burglars. Think Cary Grant in *To Catch a Thief*, and carried these little walkie-talkies—"

"It wasn't that long ago," Tal interrupted. "Why not cellphones?"

"Because it didn't go with the vibe." Marcia rolled her eyes. "So they're creeping along the walls, not looking obvious at all, and dodging in and out of doorways. Joyce kept shushing Lorna over the walkies because she was laughing so hard."

Sylvie and the others who were standing had edged closer to hear the story. Carl moved behind Sylvie and placed his hands on her waist. Bending down, he said, "Our employers lead double lives. By day, they're upstanding, church-going citizens, but at night…" His voice lowered on the last word, sending a shiver down her spine. She snuggled back against him, liking the feel of him, and liking that he was making it obvious that they were together.

Someone asked Ali about their honeymoon and how long it would be before he retired.

He grinned down at Marcia before saying, "I'm not sure if she wants me around the house all the time yet, but it won't be too much longer."

"And who's going to take your place?" Tal asked.

Ali looked at the group of younger people standing around the table. Sylvie was sure his eyes were fixed on her and Carl. "I've got some ideas," he replied.

The reception broke up soon after that, and Carl followed

Sylvie out to the parking lot. "Any chance you can give me a ride? I Ubered over after dropping Gram off."

Sylvie leaned up against her car and looked him over. "That sounds like you were planning to get carried away tonight."

"Something like that," he said, crowding her against the car door. One hand landing on the car near her shoulder, and the other on her hip, he bent to tease his lips from her temple to her jaw. "Did I tell you how beautiful you look?" He spoke in that low tone that always made her toes curl.

"I don't think so," she replied, raising her hands to press them against his chest. His shirt was unbuttoned, and she teased her thumbs against his skin.

He toyed with one thin strap of her plum colored satin dress. Betty Ann, who owned a popular boutique on Main Street, had pulled it off a rack for Sylvie. It had a low, scooped neckline, and she'd worried that she didn't have enough cleavage to do it justice or that she'd never be able to get it over her hips, but she was drawn to the subtle sheen. When she tried it on, it fit like a glove, like it had been made for her. It, along with the low-heeled strappy sandals that went with it, cost a fortune. But seeing the admiring gleam in Carl's eyes made it worth every penny.

"Well you do. You were the best-looking woman there tonight, and I couldn't keep my eyes off of you. Now, I can't keep my hands off you." He skimmed his hands down and around to cup her bottom and draw her closer. At the same time, he nipped her bottom lip, then soothed it with his tongue.

Going up on her toes, she slid her hands up his chest, splaying her fingers to dig them into the tight curls of his hair.

He groaned and deepened the kiss until she saw stars and moonbeams and rainbows. The sound of a car engine starting up brought her back to earth, and she pulled away, burying her nose in Carl's open shirt.

"We should get out of here. Where do you want me to take you?"

"Anywhere," he answered. "As long as it's with you."

CHAPTER 20

He'd twisted around in the passenger seat to stare at her as she drove, one hand resting on the back of her seat and playing with her hair. It was hard to keep her eyes open and both hands on the steering wheel when she wanted to melt into his touch, but somehow she managed to do so, and they made it back to her apartment without incident.

Hoping Carl would indeed wind up at her place, she'd spent the morning in a cleaning frenzy, and her kitchen shone. There were fresh, fluffy towels in the sparkling bathroom, vacuum tracks on the carpet, and most importantly, clean sheets on the bed. Afterward, she'd collapsed on the couch.

But then she didn't like the placement of the living room furniture, so she'd arranged and rearranged it to look cozier, and placed candles artfully around the room. To say she was nervous was an understatement. Images of Carl naked and hovering over her had haunted her dreams. She had no doubt the reality would be even better.

Part of her dream came true about twenty minutes later.

Having told Carl to get comfortable, she'd gone into the kitchen to assemble a late-night snack. From the fridge, she pulled the cheeseboard she'd assembled that morning and the wine. And not her usual box of Okanagan Porchbanger. For this momentous night—at least she hoped it would be—she'd splurged on a higher-end bottle. On a waiting tray, she arranged the cheeseboard, plates, napkins, and two glasses of wine.

Carl sat on the couch, one arm draped along the back of the cushions. She'd been right about the candles because the soft light made his dark eyes shine. Transfixed by the invitation in his smile, she walked into the living room and promptly tripped.

Moving quickly, Carl leaped from the couch to catch the falling glasses, but not before the contents splashed across his face, to drip down his chest. Cheese, crackers, cornichons, and cured meats were scattered across the coffee table that Sylvie had relocated earlier that day. Holding the two glasses, Carl blinked drops of wine from his lashes.

Sylvie's mouth hung open as she stared at him in dismay. "Oh my God! I am so, so sorry!"

"It's okay," he said, smacking his lips. "I like a good rosé." He set the glasses on the tray and took it from Sylvie's hands. "Are you okay? Did you hurt yourself?"

Pain radiated from where her knee had connected with the stupid coffee table. It wasn't bleeding, but she'd have a lovely bruise tomorrow. "No," she replied, bending her knee experimentally. "I'm fine, but your shirt isn't." Soaked through in spots, the fabric was rapidly turning pink.

He took the tray into the kitchen and returned, unbuttoning his shirt and pulling it from the waistband of his trousers. "It'll wash. But do you have a towel? I'd like to clean up a bit."

After guiding him to the bathroom and handing him a

towel, Sylvie went to clean up the mess. The good news was that nothing had broken, and only Carl had gotten wet. The bad news was…she sucked at seduction. He probably had an Uber on the way, ready to make his escape. She scooped the remains of her carefully planned evening off the coffee table and got down on her knees to retrieve tiny pickles from under the couch.

She turned to look when Carl returned, and her mouth hung open again. Hands shoved into his trouser pockets, and shirtless, he was a sight to behold. A smattering of hair covered his pectoral muscles and arrowed down his taut belly. The slopes and dips that defined the muscles of his arms and chest called to her, and she rose from the floor, knowing she was staring and not caring a bit.

"I rinsed out my shirt and hung it in the shower. It should be dry by morning," he said.

Her hands fluttered at her sides, and she clasped them together in front of her stomach. "Do you, um, want me to see if I have something that fits you?"

He shrugged as he slowly closed the gap between them. "Why bother? It will just come off in a few minutes anyway."

"It will?" she replied, swallowing the saliva that had pooled in her mouth.

"Unless we're not on the same page."

She could only blink at him stupidly.

His expression shifted to one of uncertainty. "Sylvie," he said softly. "I've wanted to make love to you for months. But I haven't pushed. First, to be sure that you wanted to as well, and second, because you were working for my grandmother. And I thought that tonight might be the night." His shoulders slumped, and he pressed his lips together, looking away. "But if I was wrong and misread—"

She was on him before he could finish the sentence, wrapping her arms around his waist and pressing her fore-head against his chest with a sigh. "You didn't misread a thing. I just wanted to make it special, and…" She flapped a hand at the mess of food and groaned.

"Babe," he said, kissing the top of her head. "It was special. I don't know that I've ever had a woman fall for me quite like that."

She whipped her head up to glare at him, and he laughed.

"How about you show me what else you've done to make tonight special. Like," he slipped a finger under the strap of her dress "if you're wearing anything special under here."

She took his hand and led him to her bedroom, where he gazed around, taking in the gauzy curtains, the collection of framed family photographs on the walls, the fluffy scatter rug, and finally, the bed.

Sylvie looked from him to the bed and back again. "Thank you for doing that for me," she said.

"I didn't think you needed to drag bad memories into your new home."

This man.

His gift had led her to replace the sheets, covers, pillows— anything that had come into contact with Dean, anything that could remind her of him. Carl's presence removed any lingering trace.

Patiently, he watched her. She sensed that if she took him to bed and asked him to hold her, and nothing else, he would do so without complaint.

She reached behind her to unzip her dress, and he said, "Let me."

When she turned around, the mirror above the dresser allowed her to watch him. His big hands cupped her shoulders, and he bent to kiss the sensitive skin behind her ear. With deft movements, he unzipped the dress and pulled it from her shoulders, catching her eyes in the mirror as the fabric lowered to the floor. His gaze turned appreciative, and the tension that had coiled within her slowly released.

Carl glided his hands down her arms and over her belly.

The belly that, despite constant workouts, refused to disappear. Its softness didn't seem to bother him, and he slid one hand across to hold her hip and the other up between her breasts, and spread his fingers to stroke against her throat and jaw.

Pulled back against his chest, the dark brown of his shoulders framed the bronze of her own in a beautiful image she wished she could capture.

"So this was what was under your dress," he said, playing with the waistband of her thong. "Did you wear it for me?"

She nodded.

He knelt to slip the thong over her hips and down her legs, lifting one foot and then the other to allow her to step out of it. Standing again, he caught her eyes in the mirror as he shoved the skimpy material in his pocket, then smoothed his hands from her rib cage over her hips to her thighs and back up again. The featherlight touch left a heat that radiated down to her toes and up to the crown of her head. Despite the warmth, she shivered and watched his hands come up to capture her breasts, holding them in his palms, his rough thumbs stroking over their tips until they tightened into dusky points.

His eyes hooded, and he shifted his hips to tease her behind with his erection, the fabric of his trousers abrading her sensitive skin in the best way. If he hadn't been holding her upright, she would have melted until all that remained was a puddle of desire. But what a way to go.

Sighing out her name, he nuzzled against the curve of her neck, nibbling and kissing along her collarbone until she tilted her head to give him more access. He took it, still slightly shocked that this bright, beautiful woman would choose him.

He hadn't lied when he told her he couldn't keep his eyes off her. And from what he'd overheard at the wedding reception, other men felt the same. One guy, who must have been a recent hire, said, "That's not Sylvie." When his companion corrected him, the guy marveled, "Talk about hiding your light under a bushel." Carl didn't think Sylvie was hiding anything; she shone every day, regardless of how she dressed.

The evenings they were able to be together were almost as much torture as their evenings apart. He'd wanted to get naked with her long before he'd kissed her the first time. But he'd wanted to be sure, to know that, without a doubt, Sylvie was over Dean and Carl was not just the rebound guy. Thinking about how much he wanted her was scary. Not just sex, but Sylvie.

So he'd held back. They'd kissed and touched, but never more than that. Every evening, he'd go home to jack off in the shower and start his day doing the same thing after dreaming about her all night long.

Now she was naked and in his arms, rubbing her spectacular ass against his rock-hard cock with so much force that if she didn't slow down, the friction alone would make him combust. Reluctantly, he released her and took a step back.

Her heavy-lidded eyes popped open, and she stared at him in confusion. "Babe," he smirked, seeing a pout forming on her luscious lips, "any chance I can take these pants off before I explode in them?"

Her gaze moved to the bulge in his trousers, and she smirked. "I think I can help with that."

Expecting her to unzip his pants, she surprised him by running her hands along the waistband to meet in the middle of his back. She stroked up his spine and around to his chest to flick his nipples. He gasped and she giggled before leaning close to take one in her mouth and sucking on it. It wasn't helping the situation in his pants, and he groaned, moving his hands to the fly to take care of things himself.

"Uh-uh," she said, playfully slapping his hands away. "That's my job."

"Then get to it, woman," he growled.

She blew a cool breath across his nipple, making it pebble in response. "In due time. You got to play, now it's my turn." She grinned and commenced playing, teasing her hands over every inch of available skin she could reach, standing on her toes the whole time to kiss him senseless. Just when he thought he'd die from toxic sperm buildup, she undid his pants to slip a hand inside. Finally! He sighed and pressed into her hand, loving the feel of it around his straining cock.

One hand wrapped around him, the other pushed his pants and briefs over his hips and down his legs, then up to grab his ass. A sizzle went up his spine, and his balls ached with the need to come. Reluctantly, he pulled her hand away. "As good as that feels, I would much rather not come right now," he said, wrestling his way out of his clothes and tossing a condom onto the bedside table.

They lay on the bed facing each other, and he drew in a shaky breath, ignoring the insistent pulse in his cock to stare at Sylvie, praying this wasn't a dream. She rubbed her thighs together, releasing the scent of her desire, and he gently pushed her back to slide down her, leaving a trail of kisses in his wake. Her body trembled, and she clutched at the sheets as he hovered above her sex.

His biceps flexed as he lowered himself to nudge her mound with his nose, inhaling a scent that was uniquely Sylvie. He slicked the tip of his tongue slowly along her seam, coming close to her clit but pulling back, wanting to torture her the same way she'd tortured him.

She sank her fingers into his hair and pulled him against her, legs splayed in invitation. He accepted gladly, licking and sucking on her clit, taking her to the edge and pulling back repeatedly until her thighs tightened around him. Convul-

sions went through her in waves, and she sighed her satisfaction.

"Come here," she said, releasing her grip on his hair.

He was happy to obey, rising up to lie on his side next to
her, his cock bobbing against her leg, begging for attention. It
would be a challenge, but if she didn't want anything more
this evening, he'd settle for the look in her eyes, knowing
that he'd put it there.

Her eyes locked on his, she took his cock in her hand,
stroking her thumb over the precum that leaked from his
crown. Closing his eyes, he willed himself to hold out a little
longer, then opened them at the distinct sound of crinkling
foil. She sheathed the condom over his length and spread her
legs wide. Wordlessly, he shifted to cover her body with his
own, watching her the whole time.

He pressed against her entrance, then slid inside in one
smooth push. Her hands on his shoulders, she wrapped her
legs around his waist, holding him tight as he began to move.
"Hang on," he grunted. "I don't know how long I can last."

"Then don't," she replied, squeezing her inner muscles
around him.

"Are you sure?"

"Yeah." She tilted her pelvis up and guided one of his
hands to her slick folds. Obligingly, he teased her clit,
watching her eyelashes flutter and her lips part. She let out a
low moan that he felt down to his toes. "Perfect," she
murmured.

And it was. He rocked against her, picking up speed until
her tits bounced, the bed shook, and they were both
drenched in sweat. By some miracle, he held off until Sylvie's
face flushed as her orgasm rippled through her. Then he let
go, flooding the condom with his release and collapsing over
her to bury his face in her neck.

When he was able to breathe again, he kissed her long

and deep, then got up to deal with the condom. She was still in the same spot when he returned, but she was watching him, her fingers curling in invitation. Carl climbed back into bed to take her into his arms, loving the sound of her sighs as she settled against him.

CHAPTER 21

A few nights later, the remains of their takeout dinner lay scattered across the coffee table, and Sylvie was straddling Carl's lap, his hands gripping her behind. Her shirt and bralette had been discarded along with the pad Thai, and she held his head in place as he nuzzled first one breast and then the other. She hummed with pleasure and rolled her hips, anticipating more.

He let go and looked up at her. "Your ass is vibrating."

"Um-hmm, so are other parts of me."

"Babe, no. It's your phone."

She huffed out a sigh and retrieved her phone from her back pocket, then froze in place. "Crap. It's Tomas."

"What?" Carl looked wildly around the room, like he suspected her brother was watching them through a hidden camera.

Sylvie rolled her eyes as she engaged the call. "Hey, what's up?"

"It's Burrito Bonanza night, and you're late," Tomas replied.

"Already?" She mouthed an apology at Carl as she clambered off him to look for her clothes. "I'll be there as soon as I can."

"And bring Carl. Many hands and all that stuff."

"How did you know he's here?"

"I didn't. You just told me," Tomas replied and disconnected.

"What's going on?" Carl asked, rising from the couch as she donned first her bralette and then her top.

"I forgot that tonight is Burrito Bonanza at the church, and I need to go and help out. You're welcome to come too."

"Okay, but I'm going to need a bit more of an explanation."

Together, they cleaned up after their meal, and Sylvie told him about the monthly meal preparation assembly line at the church. A group gathered each month in the church's commercial kitchen to prepare, package, and deliver food. Some of it went to local shelters, some of it went to the senior center, and some was delivered directly to families and individuals who weren't able to leave their homes.

"And your family does it every month?" Carl asked. He loaded the dishwasher, then wiped down the counter, as if doing the dishes with her was something they'd done a thousand times.

"No. We do it four times a year." She twisted her hands together, wishing they were back on the couch and she hadn't ruined their evening. "It'll take a couple of hours, and you don't have to come. You can hang out here and watch TV until I get back."

"I don't mind," he said, turning to take her hands. "Besides, your brother will give me shit if I don't show up."

Laughing, she grabbed her keys and phone and locked the door behind them.

Carl grabbed her hips and pulled her back to whisper in her ear. "And you're worth the wait."

"Whoa," Carl said as they entered the church kitchen. The big island in the center was flanked on each side with a ton of people: Tomas and Fiona, Vincent and Hilary, Pastor Andy and Joseph Han, Cara and her partner Sierra. All gloved up and wearing aprons, they were indeed working in an assembly line.

Large tortillas, which Sylvie had said were made in her mother's restaurant, were piled up in front of Fiona. She placed a few in front of Cara, who spread a scoop of meat mixture over each one before sliding it to Hilary. She topped it with cheese, then slid it to Sierra, who added chopped tomatoes. Sierra then deftly rolled up the burrito and added it to a tray filled with finished burritos.

Vincent headed up a similar production line on the opposite side of the island, with Joseph at his side, followed by Pastor Andy, and Tomas at the end.

Pastor Andy looked up at their entrance and raised his hands skyward. "Reinforcements! Thank you, Jesus!"

A chorus of "amens" came from the other workers, who all smiled and nodded at Carl and Sylvie.

"I am so sorry," Sylvie said as she dragged Carl to the handwashing station. "We had dinner and then got caught up in—"

Tomas cut her off, raising an admonishing eyebrow. "I don't want to know."

"Conversation!" Sylvie said, shooting him a narrow-eyed look. "We were talking."

Hilary turned to Sierra and mused, "Is that what the kids are calling it these days?"

Carl pumped soap into his hands and set about scrubbing them, hoping his face wouldn't be red when he looked up. He hadn't expected to see his boss, but he should have. Tomas and Vincent were tight, so it stood to reason that their spouses would be present as well.

Sylvie's cheeks had gone an adorable shade of pink, but she appeared to take the ribbing in stride, asking, "Where do you want us?"

There was a shuffling of positions, and Carl wound up standing beside Pastor Andy at the short end of the island, both of them assigned to wrap the burritos in cling wrap. Neither were particularly proficient, and it took them a minute to figure out a system, but they got there. Gradually, the tray of wrapped burritos filled up, and Carl felt like he was making a valuable contribution.

"This must feel familiar to you," Andy—he'd insisted that calling him Pastor Andy wasn't necessary—said.

"Uh, no. I have never wrapped burritos in my life."

Andy gestured to their surroundings. "I mean, prepping food in here." Seeing Carl's confused expression, he added, "Your grandmother started this outreach many years ago. Didn't you ever get roped into helping?"

"Not once," Carl replied. "It's possible my sister did, though." A twinge of guilt hit him at his inability to recall Gram mentioning it. No doubt he hadn't bothered listening, too focused on whatever his teenage brain was fixated on. He made a mental note to ask her about it the next time he visited.

"Do all the local restaurants participate?" Carl asked.

"Nope. Youth groups, scout troops, and service organizations are also involved. Our church is where the food is prepped because we're centrally located and we have the best equipment."

Carl looked at the aging appliances and scarred countertops, secretly disagreeing about the last bit. One cupboard door was completely missing, and duct tape was applied in multiple places. Mentally, he created a list of supplies to make the repairs, wondering if he should do it himself or check with Vincent and Tomas. Maybe he could bring a couple of Keeney Build students with him.

"Earth calling Carl," Andy's voice brought him back to the present. "Where were you?"

"Figuring the cost of updating this kitchen and wondering why it hasn't been done sooner."

"Because there are greater needs in the community," the group chorused in a monotone, like they'd heard the phrase more times than they could count.

"I get that," Carl replied, "but aren't we Keeney Building Supply? Fixing this place up wouldn't cost much or take a lot of time." Seeing the pained expressions on the faces around him, he asked, "What am I missing?"

"Politics," Andy replied.

"In a church kitchen? You're kidding me."

"Oh, to be that young and innocent," Vincent said with an overly dramatic sigh, and the others laughed good-naturedly.

The work moved from preparing and packaging the burritos to putting them into large, labeled coolers, which would be picked up by volunteer delivery drivers shortly. The group then proceeded to clean the kitchen. Carl could see that, despite its worn condition, it was well-organized and scrupulously clean. Andy told him about the stalemate as pots were scrubbed and surfaces were sanitized.

A woman who had been a dedicated kitchen volunteer left a tidy sum of money to the church, designated explicitly for updating the kitchen. Everyone was excited until it was discovered that there was a stipulation: the woman's two daughters needed to sign off on the plans before funds could be accessed.

"Is that normal?" Carl asked.

"Not at all," Andy replied. "We're used to people leaving money to the church for specific purposes, like funding maintenance of the pipe organ or structural repairs, but no one from the family goes over the receipts. And if they did, it wouldn't be an issue. The Dawson sisters, like their mother, regularly volunteer in the kitchen, so they are well aware of the needs, and we assumed that the updates would have been made long ago.

"The problem is that they can't agree on the plans. One is extremely cautious and wants to make only the necessary repairs as they arise. The other wants to do a whole kitchen remodel and get it over and done with. And until they can come to an agreement, we're stuck.

"To make matters worse, they're both on the facilities team and will only agree to repairs in the kitchen if we can't find a workaround, hence the liberal use of duct tape. Because of their attitudes, no one in the church is willing to serve on that committee anymore." Frustration leaked through Andy's words, and he scrubbed at the countertop with short, jerky movements.

Joseph wrapped an arm around his husband. "Breathe, sweetheart. Getting worked up won't do you any good." He pressed his lips together in a tight smile as he looked at Carl. "In preparation for meeting with the Dawsons, he pops antacids hours in advance and I queue up reruns of *Glee* for him to zone out to when he gets home."

Carl propped a hip against the counter and crossed his arms. "What you do in this space is something to be proud of. It's a shame you can't be proud of the space itself." He bent down and picked a piece of broken Formica off the corner of a drawer. "I'm surprised this program hasn't found a different location to prepare the food. One that isn't falling down around the volunteers while they work."

Andy looked at him and nodded. Then his back straightened, his eyes widened, and he smiled broadly. Carl could practically see the lightbulb go on above his head.

"That's it!" Andy grabbed Carl's arm. "Come with me." He dragged Carl out of the kitchen, through the fellowship hall, and out into the main hallway. They stopped outside a small conference room where four people were gathered around a table. A murmur of voices could be heard through the open door.

"Follow my lead," Andy told him. "And say exactly what you did in the kitchen." Carl bobbed his head, and Andy went on, speaking loudly, "Thanks for helping out tonight with preparing the food. We really appreciate new volunteers."

"Any time," Carl replied.

Andy waited, then rolled his eyes and his hands at the same time. "And what did you think?"

"It's a good program."

Andy jerked his head toward the conference room, whispering, "The Dawson sisters are in there. Let them hear what you told me."

The same lightbulb went on over Carl's head, and he practically shouted, "I think it's great that organizations gather here and use your kitchen to prepare and distribute food to the community. The meals program is something to be really proud of. It's a shame you can't be proud of the space itself."

"Why do you say that?"

He and Andy stood behind the open door, out of view of the people in the room, which had gone silent. "Isn't it embarrassing to have groups come into your church and see the disrepair in the kitchen? Especially because it wouldn't cost much to fix it. Even if you were to do a complete overhaul. It's surprising that the entire program hasn't relocated to a kitchen that isn't falling down around them."

"That would be a shame if that happened," Andy sounded mournful but looked gleeful. "Our church is invested in the program. But if it needs a better kitchen to function, I'd rather the program relocate than have it end."

Carl heaved a dramatic sigh. "I'd hate to have to tell my grandmother that. She put a lot of effort into getting it going."

Giving him a thumbs up, Andy asked, "How is Miss Jean doing these days?" as they walked away.

The others were still waiting in the kitchen, staring at them with bemused expressions, and Joseph pointed an accusing finger at his husband. "I know that look. What kind of scheme have you conjured up?"

"Nothing," Andy replied, the picture of innocence.

Joseph narrowed his eyes, but the sound of running feet prevented him from asking more questions.

Two gray-haired women burst through the doorway, all but hyperventilating with panic and babbling about not wanting to lose the meals program.

Andy patted the air. "Ladies, please, slow down. I don't know what you're talking about."

Carl covered his mouth and faked a cough to cover up the giggle rising inside him.

The woman with the blue hair took a deep breath and explained that she and her sister wanted to release the funds their mother had left to the church. The other woman, this one with tight salt and pepper curls, nodded eagerly, saying, "All of it. Use all of it to make this kitchen the best it can be. A space to be proud of!"

"Are you absolutely sure?" Andy asked, feigning surprise.

"We're sure," they said in unison.

"And you don't need to weigh in on each individual item?"

They shook their heads so hard Carl was sure they would injure themselves.

After that, Joseph offered suggestions for the wording, and Andy scratched out an agreement to release the funds. With Fiona acting as a witness, the two women, whom Carl assumed were the Dawson sisters, signed immediately and then left, looking relieved yet slightly shellshocked.

When the women were no longer in sight, Joseph poked

Andy again with a finger. "Spill. What did you do to make that happen?"

"Not here," Andy replied, ushering everyone out of the church and into the farthest corner of the parking lot, where, in hushed tones and with much dramatization, he explained about the conversation in the corridor.

"Well done, dude," Vincent said, smacking Carl on the shoulder. "Mom will be thrilled."

"Your mom?" Sylvie scoffed. "My mom will hold a parade in your honor. She says she breaks out in hives every time she walks into that kitchen."

It was beginning to dawn on Carl that his casual observations had made a bunch of people happy. Scratch that, he thought when Andy smacked kisses on both of his cheeks. These people were ecstatic.

*S*nuggled down in Sylvie's bed, Carl pressed a kiss to her bare shoulder and nuzzled behind her ear, anticipating the pleasurable moments it would lead up to.

"Uh-uh," she said, poking him in the ribs. "Not until you tell me the full story."

"But you already know the story," he protested.

"And we've already had sex," she countered. "So if you want it again tonight, you'll have to tell me the story."

"Fiiiiine." He rolled to his back and drew her against his side, loving the way she fit so snugly. Sylvie had been washing dishes and hadn't heard his conversation with Andy in the kitchen, so he described that, and then Andy dragging him to repeat the conversation out of sight, but in hearing range of the people in the conference room. "It took me a minute to clue into what he was up to," Carl confessed.

Sylvie snorted. "Who knew our mild-mannered pastor was so Machiavellian. But you—" she raised up to kiss him hard on the mouth "—you were the hero."

"I just said what everyone was thinking."

"But you said it at the right time, to the right person, and in the right place."

He opened his mouth to protest further, but she stopped him with a finger against his lips. "Accept it. You done good. And all the people of Keeney are grateful."

Her voice had gone throaty, and he became aware of her hand gliding in slow, expanding circles across his chest, over his ribs, and down his belly. His cock stood at attention as her hand got closer.

"How grateful?" he rasped out.

"Very," she whispered between kisses as she took hold of his cock, tugging and stroking until his eyes rolled back in his head. He didn't care if all of Keeney was grateful. He was just happy that Sylvie was happy.

CHAPTER 22

$\mathcal{A}$rms crossed, Carl watched Ingrid handle the chop saw with the respect it deserved. She was cautious but not afraid, a trait that would serve her well around power tools capable of removing body parts. She finished the cuts, powered off, and stood back to look at him.

He held up two thumbs. "That's it. You've successfully demonstrated all of the saws. I'll have to check with Ali, but I think that's the quickest any of our employees has done so. Too bad we don't give out report cards, because you'd have all As."

She glowed under the praise. Despite the sucky circumstances surrounding her arrival, she'd become quite the asset at KBS. Many of the store employees were happy to simply sell the tools, but Ingrid had wanted to learn how to operate them and what tasks each was best suited for.

"Hey, you're wanted in the conference room," another KBS employee called.

"Me?" Carl pointed at his chest.

"Both of you."

Ingrid and Carl looked at each other, shrugged, and headed to the offices. Ali and Marcia were off on their honeymoon—a trip to Eastern Canada, and Carl was filling in for Ali in his absence. He'd expected resistance from some of the employees who'd been there longer than him, but no one on the loading dock had blinked twice. He'd also asked Ali why he hadn't approached Sylvie, who seemed like the logical choice. "I did," Ali replied. "But she laughed in my face and said, 'Not on your life.'"

The job offer for marketing director was still on the table because Carl had some ideas and had told Ali they'd talk when he returned. Caught up in wedded bliss, Ali acquiesced easily, and so far, KBS was running smoothly.

Carl stood aside to allow Ingrid to enter the conference room first, nearly plowing into her when she stopped suddenly.

"Hey! What the—oh." Peering over Ingrid's shoulder, he saw an unfamiliar man and Ron Sanchez sitting at the conference table. Sylvie sat opposite them while Hilary occupied her usual chair at the head of the table.

Hilary waved them in, pointing for them to have a seat, but Ingrid didn't move.

Carl stepped around her, saying, "You okay?"

She took a deep breath, nodded, and moved to the chair farthest from the visitors. Carl sat beside Sylvie, shooting her a quizzical glance. She shrugged, shaking her head. Hilary introduced the KBS employees to the man, a plainclothes detective with the Keeney Police, who gave his name as Frank Tsing.

Dean's father looked like he was carrying the weight of the world on his shoulders. Purple bruising under bloodshot eyes told the tale of sleepless nights. Impeccably dressed in a sport coat and open-collared dress shirt, his hand shook when he picked up a coffee cup, and there was a tiny nick under his jaw where he'd cut himself shaving.

The cop had a stack of folders and an open notebook in front of him. Writing down each person's name and their position at KBS, he then pulled two papers out of a folder and turned them so that Sylvie, Carl, and Ingrid could read them.

"These are KBS invoices recording sales of lumber to Sanchez Homes. Can you confirm their accuracy?" Detective Tsing asked.

"Sylvie," Hilary said. "Please pull our copies and print them out."

Sylvie went to her desk, and Carl asked, "What's this about?"

The cop glanced at Ron Sanchez with a seemingly sympathetic look before answering. "We arrested Dean Sanchez yesterday morning at a warehouse in Duvall. It was filled to the rafters with building supplies stolen from Sanchez Homes."

Sylvie's desk was behind the cop, and she'd been tapping at her computer keyboard. Her fingers froze, and she glanced up at Carl. Her eyes were filled with the same shock and surprise that held him immobile. The moment passed, and Sylvie pressed a button; a printer started up. She brought over the papers and handed them to Detective Tsing.

"Are they the same?" Hilary asked.

Detective Tsing studied the invoices, pointed something out to Ron Sanchez, and said, "No. The cost is the same, but the amount of goods is different." He tapped the original paper. "Sanchez Homes received significantly less than what KBS says was delivered."

"May I see those?" Sylvie asked. Accepting them, she and Hilary put their heads together to examine them closely.

As Ali's proxy, Carl knew why he was there. Sylvie's and Hilary's presence was a given, but why Ingrid? He watched her out of the corner of his eye, noting her stiff posture and that she was staring down at her hands.

Sylvie murmured something, and Hilary nodded. "I see it," she said.

"Detective Tsing, we updated our invoices about four months ago, adding a new logo beneath the company name." She pointed to the words, "Building Community," written in a smaller font beneath "Keeney Building Supply."

"This order is dated six weeks ago, yet it's on the outdated invoice form. It's been forged. We can prove that by reviewing our delivery records. They're entered into the system separately from the invoice. The yard receives the order and fills out the delivery form accordingly. It's a security measure KBS implemented to prevent theft on our end." Her voice softened as she addressed Dean's father, "I'm sorry, Mr. Sanchez."

He dipped his head, accepting her words like they weren't a surprise.

Sylvie slipped into the chair beside Carl, capturing his hand and giving it a squeeze. He squeezed back. Dean Sanchez was going down, and he couldn't be happier. However, now was not the time to celebrate.

Detective Tsing asked a few more questions and secured the KBS invoices. He stated that the police would also be examining invoices from other building supply companies.

"How did you find out about this?" Carl asked.

Ron Sanchez spoke for the first time. "An envelope was delivered to my office containing printouts of screenshots taken of Dean's computer and ledger pages. The highlighted items indicated sources of income." He looked at Sylvie. "I taught my son to keep meticulous records, and that will be his undoing. He recorded the transfers he made from your account." He switched his gaze to Ingrid. "He recorded how he gained access to the account as well. I am so sorry for the damage he caused you both."

Sylvie squeezed Carl's hand tighter, but said only, "Thank you, Mr. Sanchez."

Ingrid smiled slightly and bobbed her head, but didn't say anything.

Ron Sanchez gave them all one last nod before standing and pushing in his chair. He seemed to have aged a decade in less than a minute. Being victimized by your own family would do that to a person, though. Carl hoped it would never happen to him.

Hilary rose with the two men and walked them out of the conference room.

When their footsteps receded, Sylvie high-fived Carl. "Yes!" she whisper-shouted.

Color had returned to Ingrid's face, and she'd unclenched her hands. "Good," she said.

Carl swiveled in his chair, glad to have all that behind them. "I wonder, though," he said, "who took the pictures and sent them to Dean's father?"

"I don't know," Sylvie replied. "But I want to give them a big hug.

"The asshat always preached at me about the importance of good bookkeeping and how I'd have to do a better job when we started our business. It looks like he screwed himself. Hah!"

The office phone rang, and she went to answer it. Carl took that as a sign to get back to work and walked to the door, Ingrid following behind him. "Come in here," he said, pointing to the open door of Ali's office.

Once inside, he sat in one of the two chairs facing Ali's desk.

"Why aren't you sitting in Ali's chair? You're doing his job these days," Ingrid said, taking the other chair.

Carl shuddered. "Yeah, no. Sitting at his desk feels weird. I don't mind doing the work, but I will never be Ali."

"I don't know if it's common knowledge, but Marcia is stepping down." Seeing Ingrid's surprised expression, he went on, "Yeah, she wants to do more volunteering. Ali offered me the marketing director position, and while I think

I can do it, I believe there's a better person for the position. And *that person* is you."

Her mouth hung open as she stared at him.

"Don't look so surprised," Carl said. "Other than the crap with Dean, you have a good resume, and I've heard the ideas you've shared with Sylvie and Hilary."

"But…but Ali offered the job to you."

"That's because you've been flying under his radar, and he's been wrapped up in the wedding and didn't notice you. Is the position something you'd be interested in?"

She was nodding before he finished the question.

"Good. I can only make a recommendation, but be prepared to make a presentation."

"I will make a presentation that will knock Ali's socks off!" Grinning like she'd just won the lottery, Ingrid bopped up out of her chair and danced down the hallway.

Carl leaned back in his chair and stretched, mentally ticking an item off his to-do list. The list was getting shorter and shorter, and he'd soon be free of the obligations that prevented him from moving on. He couldn't wait.

*S*ylvie sat at her kitchen table that evening, looking at real estate listings, with a cup of tea to her left and a notebook to her right, next to her laptop. Part of the reason renovating and selling Miss Jean's house had gone so well was that she knew in advance that it would be up for sale. In an open market, she couldn't have successfully bid on the house, and she needed an edge for future purchases.

Fiona's family owned commercial real estate through Han Family Holdings, so at her suggestion, Sylvie reached out to Joseph and Andy. As the pastor at Keeney UMC, Andy had an in with many retirees in Keeney, some of whom would be interested in selling their homes and moving into retirement communities. At the wedding reception, Sylvie had explained to Andy that while flipping houses that could be retrofitted for accessibility was the goal, renovating houses so people could age in them was also desirable.

So Sylvie scrolled through Google Earth, viewing images of houses that would soon be on the market, while thinking about Carl and looking forward to discussing what she found with him. Being with him was easy. He made her laugh, he made her think, he made her feel alive. He wasn't nearly as self-centered or profit-motivated as Dean and didn't scoff at her ideas.

She had a habit of processing things aloud, which had annoyed Dean, but Carl let her ramble, asking the occasional question but never trying to "fix" things for her. That was a good thing, because Sylvie hated being fixed almost as much as she hated needing to be fixed.

She knew that no one was completely perfect, and given enough time, Carl would expose a flaw. But she didn't think it would be anything they couldn't overcome.

Their schedules hadn't allowed any time together since the Burrito Bonanza. After full days at KBS, she'd been mudding and taping most evenings. Then she'd come home, shower, and, after exchanging—sometimes steamy—text messages with Carl, she'd crash.

Now that Dean was firmly out of the picture—and being measured for an orange jumpsuit—the sun shone brighter every day. This wasn't exactly how she'd planned to start her business, but she was happy with how it had turned out.

In the break room that morning, Carl cornered her for a kiss that practically steamed up the windows. He'd told her that he needed to make a trip down to Olympia so he wouldn't see her until tomorrow evening, and it couldn't come fast enough. She'd already figured out what she'd wear but couldn't decide what to do with her hair.

She'd been watching YouTube videos about hair styling

and wanted to try an elaborate updo. He loved her hair, seeming to take a particular pleasure in releasing it from her usual ponytails. And she loved the look he'd get in his eyes, all smoldery and...a shiver ran through her, and she squirmed in her chair.

Sex with Carl was fabulous. Alternating between slow and gentle and hard and fast, but never rough. That wasn't something either of them wanted. He checked in with her about everything: her needs, her pace, her fulfillment. If they never had sex again, she'd still have a host of memories to keep her going for a lifetime. But that wouldn't be the case because he would be with her in less than twenty-four hours, and she planned to have him naked shortly after that.

When they had met three years ago, he'd been cute, earnest, and eager. No doubt dating him would have been fun, but would they have lasted? Would they have developed the same connection they'd made over the past few months? She'd never know, so there was no point in dwelling on it.

What she did know was that the cocky attitude he'd returned to Keeney with had dissipated as he dealt with his grandmother's situation. While Sylvie had assisted with the tangible aspects of the house and getting Miss Jean settled into the assisted living facility, Carl hadn't shared much about his feelings. He'd grumbled a bit about his mother micromanaging through phone calls and emails, and Sylvie had been happy to listen. But she would have also been happy to listen if he'd shared about the difficulty of discovering Miss Jean had congestive heart failure, because she knew how much his grandmother meant to him.

Carl had been there for her through the shitshow that was Dean's betrayal. There'd been no judgment, simply support.

And ice cream. She couldn't forget the ice cream.

Now, she wanted the opportunity to be there for him, to

be supportive and buy him ice cream, and to kiss him at every opportunity.

A rap at the door roused Sylvie from her pleasant thoughts. Ingrid was bouncing on her toes so hard, Sylvie thought she'd go through the floorboards.

"What's up?" she asked, waving her inside.

Ingrid burst through the door, squealing like a little girl. "I have the best news! Carl's going to recommend me for Marcia's job."

She went on about needing to make a presentation and wondering what she should wear, oblivious to Sylvie's silence.

Carl was passing on the marketing job at KBS. *Was he not staying in Keeney? Is that why he was down in Olympia?* He must have gotten the job in Alaska, and they were working out the details.

She slumped against the counter, fixed a smile in place, and made encouraging noises at Ingrid. Her enthusiasm couldn't be contained, and she paced Sylvie's living room, babbling about ideas before bopping back outside and down the stairs, her feet barely touching the ground.

Sylvie closed the door, staring out at the blue sky and fluffy clouds that seemed to mock her. He'd said he would *consider* staying. That's all. And they hadn't talked about it since that first conversation, she'd just assumed. And she hadn't questioned why he was staying at a short-term rental, rather than looking for an apartment.

The job at KBS wasn't worth sticking around for. She wasn't worth sticking around for. The worst of it was that he couldn't be bothered to tell her himself.

Or was that what tomorrow night would be about? Tell her in public so she wouldn't make a scene. Well, screw him. She went through her notebook looking for tomorrow's to-do list and tore it out. He wasn't worth the effort of an elaborate updo.

$\mathcal{C}$arl hummed along to the Dionne Warwick song playing softly in the background, knowing he'd be singing about San Jose in his head for the rest of the day. He'd told his grandmother he'd take her to lunch at any restaurant in Keeney, but she'd chosen the dining room at Cascades Lodge, saying she wouldn't have to get in and out of the car that way.

On the walk from her apartment to the dining room, they'd stopped frequently. Gram either introduced him to friends or pointed things out to him, like the library where she played competitive Scrabble in the evenings and the hair salon where she had a standing weekly appointment to have her hair washed. Despite needing a walker, Gram looked good and appeared to be in good spirits. She'd obviously settled in well, and he was thankful for her foresight in making the arrangements, as well as for the smooth transition.

Other than a few staff members, he was the only one under the age of forty in the dining room, where they were served meatloaf and mashed potatoes—Carl receiving an extra slice of meatloaf and a wink from their server. The food was surprisingly good, and he cleaned his plate in no time.

"Your parents will be back soon, freeing you of your burden," Gram said, sipping her tea.

"You aren't a burden," he replied truthfully. A few months ago, he'd thought that way, but a lot had changed, like being with Sylvie when the new owners arrived at his grandmother's house to pick up the keys and do a walk-through. The excitement on the daughter's face as she wheeled her walker up the ramp was surpassed only when she discovered the bathroom with the walk-in shower. Carl had been a part of making that happen, and it filled him with pride.

His phone buzzed with a call from Build Clean. Knowing how his grandmother felt about cellphones in general and taking calls at the dinner table, he turned the ringer off and shoved the phone into his pocket. All the important stuff had been taken care of, and Build Clean could wait.

Being a fly on the conference room wall when his boss and the other executives learned about Dean's arrest would have been epic. He'd tried to warn them that Dean was bad news, but all they'd seen were the dollar signs a deal with Sanchez Homes would bring them. Now they were busy pointing fingers at each other, laying the blame on whoever thought schmoozing Dean instead of going directly to his father was a good idea.

The server brought around plates of apple crisp topped with vanilla ice cream, setting one before Carl before he could refuse. Gram declined hers and requested more tea. When he finished eating, she put her cup down and said, "I have something for you in my apartment."

Carl helped her out of her chair and shortened his stride to keep pace with her on the way to the elevator. Again, Gram introduced him to everyone they passed, further lengthening the trip.

Two people lounged against the wall across from Gram's

apartment, and it took Carl a moment to recognize his parents.

"Monica?" Gram asked, sounding pleased. "I wasn't expecting you today."

"We were able to get an earlier flight," his mom explained, kissing Gram on the cheek.

She turned to Carl for an awkward embrace, surprising the hell out of him because his mother was not an affectionate woman.

Looking him over, she patted his arm. "You look well."

"You too," he said.

Monica Ryder's wardrobe was all about function. She favored khaki cargo pants, navy T-shirts, and khaki field jackets. Her wedding ring and gold hoop earrings were her only adornments; her dark hair was cropped close to her head, and he knew her skincare routine consisted of sunscreen and lip balm.

Gram, in her floral blouse, purple slacks, pearl earrings, and necklace, looked like a peacock beside her daughter.

Smiling, Danny Ryder kissed his mother-in-law on the cheek and clapped a hand on Carl's shoulder. Not as tall as Carl, his curly gray hair was beginning to recede, and his stomach expanded slightly under his olive-green T-shirt.

Chatting the whole time, Gram ushered everyone inside, and Monica and Danny toured the comfortable apartment before sitting on the couch. Gram sat in her easy chair, and Carl brought over a kitchen chair to join the conversation, which turned out to be more like an interrogation.

It was rather galling to report to his mother about renovating and selling Gram's house. She questioned again the decision to make the home accessible, stating that they'd reduced its market value. When she wanted to know the contractor's pedigree and the cost of the improvements, Carl had had enough.

"It's done, Mom. What is your point?"

Monica sniffed. "I think you made some hasty decisions. Your grandmother needed that income to live on, and I don't think you took that into consideration. I—"

"You. Weren't. Here. You told me to take care of things, and I did. Nothing was done in haste, and Gram was part of every decision made and—" he clamped his mouth shut, willing the familiar bitterness away.

After signing a new work contract, his mother would take off, rarely communicating while overseas, and then criticize Carl's movements while she was away. His father would try to smooth things over, but never stood up to his wife, never stood up for Carl.

He should have been prepared, but like his grandmother, he hadn't expected to see them until the next day.

Sensing his frustration, Gram said, "No one took advantage of me. I have more than enough to live on, and I am happy with the way things turned out. Now let it go, Monica."

His mother opened her mouth to protest, but his father put a hand on her arm to stop her, saying, "It's been a long day, and we still need to check in to the hotel. Why don't we do that? I'll pour you a glass of wine, and you can have a bath."

"Fine," she said and stood from the couch.

Gram stayed in her chair while Carl walked his parents to the door, relieved that they were leaving.

"When do you leave for Alaska?" his dad asked.

"I'm not."

His mother gaped at him. "What?"

"I'm staying in Keeney."

"You are?" His mother's voice rose an octave. "But we decided that this was a good career move. Keeney is a dead end. You can't possibly go anywhere if you stay here. What's changed?" Alarm settled over his mother's features, and she pushed past him to get to Gram.

"Are you okay? Is Carl staying here because your heart is worsening?"

Gram patted her daughter's hand. "I'm fine. This is the first I've heard about Carl planning to stay. Although I must say, that makes me very happy. Breaking my hip was a pretty dramatic way to get him to come back here, but it's worked out well. I hadn't realized how much I missed having him around."

A pang of guilt flashed through Carl. He'd put his career and the job at Build Clean first, shooting off texts to Gram instead of phoning her. Spending his free time working or trying to get ahead with his coworkers instead of driving up from Olympia for a visit. She never protested, always pleased to hear the job was going well, and he'd laugh off her comments about needing to find a personal life.

Monica jutted out her jaw. "We're not leaving for our next job for two weeks, so we'll be around too."

His father sighed so softly Carl almost missed it. "Where are you going?" he asked.

"Houston," Danny murmured, his mouth in a tight line.

"You don't like Texas?"

"I don't like big cities and I'm tired of living out of a suitcase."

Carl twisted around to face his father fully. His parents had traveled for contract work for as long as he could remember, and this was the first time Danny Ryder had ever complained. "Why don't you say something?"

His father shrugged, propping one shoulder against the wall of the entry. Carl looked over his shoulder, but his mother and grandmother had their heads together, not paying any attention to him and his father.

"Your mother loves it, and I love her." He pulled at his olive-green T-shirt. "I can put up with wearing a uniform if it means I get to be by her side. It may not seem like it, but your mother *is* worried about Gram. We won't be taking any more overseas contracts and will only accept contracts in locations with good airport access so we can get back here if needed."

Carl accepted that. It was about the best he could hope for from his mother.

Danny switched the subject. "Are you staying in Keeney for yourself?"

Sylvie's face flashed through his mind, and the tension leaked out of him. Her eyes lighting up when she saw him brightened his day, and when they'd danced at Marcia's wedding, she'd fit so snugly in his arms he hadn't wanted to let her go. It had been hard to leave her after the evening working in the church kitchen together. But both of them had obligations that couldn't be put off, and the past week of furtive kisses and text messages wasn't enough.

Her energy and passion for doing things right and for the right reason were addictive. She was a connector who put things together and made things better. She'd made *him* better. And he wanted to be better for her. He didn't regret not moving faster, and if it had been someone else, someone who didn't mean as much to him, he would have. She was tough as nails on the surface, and it would probably surprise others that she had a vulnerable side. Her revealing that vulnerability to him had been an honor. One he didn't take lightly.

"Yeah," he replied.

His father's eyes narrowed, but Carl didn't look away. He had nothing to hide.

The corner of Danny's mouth lifted as he said, "I see. I'll keep your mother off your back then. Will we get to meet her?"

"I never said there was someone."

His father snorted. "Sure. Whatever you say."

His parents said their goodbyes, leaving Carl alone with his grandmother.

He kissed her cheek and said, "If you don't need anything else, Gram, I'll get going."

Gram pushed herself up from the chair, saying, "Hang on for a moment."

She retrieved an envelope from her purse and handed it to him.

"What's this?"

"Open it," she replied, smiling like the Cheshire Cat.

He pulled out a check with a lot of numbers on it and stared at his grandmother in bemusement.

"That's your share from the sale of the house. Mandy will receive hers soon, too." She chuckled as Carl continued to stare dumbly at her. "Despite what your mother thinks, I'm not going to need it. And it would give me great pleasure to see what you do with it."

She returned to her chair, and Carl sank onto the couch, his mind reeling.

"I won't tell you what to do with it. However, I know a young builder who might be interested in a partner."

He jerked his head up. "Sylvie?"

Gram wagged a finger at him. "Now don't play dumb. I've seen the way you look at her. That girl has her head on straight and is going places. And I think she'd like you to go with her. Provided you aren't leaving Keeney."

Carl grinned. "Is this a bribe for me to stay in Keeney?"

She sniffed. "Maybe. Is it working?"

He gathered her in a gentle hug, kissing her cheek. "Thank you Gram. I love you big time."

"I love you too. But you didn't answer my question."

"We'll see." He winked and headed out the door.

CHAPTER 24

$\mathcal{I}$t shouldn't have surprised Sylvie that her mother knew the family who bought Miss Jean's house. Between her restaurant, food truck, and her church, Louisa Santiago made connections everywhere she went. She was an energetic presence and was always ready to help others, including carrying and unpacking boxes.

Sylvie hadn't intended to help the family move in, but somehow she was there. She, her father, and Cara unloaded the U-Haul and delivered boxes to their labeled destinations. The new owner was a single mom with an energetic eight-year-old boy and an eleven-year-old girl who'd been badly injured in the car accident that had killed their father. The girl, Freya, used a walker because she had balance issues and one foot dragged behind her. That didn't slow her down, though, and she zipped up and down the ramp and through the house, getting in the way more than she was being helpful.

Sylvie's mother stood to the side as Freya scooted past her on the front porch and into the house, then Louisa descended the ramp, trailing one hand along the railing. "You did this," she said, hugging Sylvie hard. "I'm so proud of you."

"Did you see the kitchen?" Cara asked. "It's got drawers instead of cupboards and is wide enough that Freya's not going to bump into anything."

Sylvie beamed under their praise. Doubly so since she knew they'd thought she was crazy to put her money into flipping houses.

"I told my Bible study group about this, and Dottie Winters wants you to come to her house. She wants you to install a ramp for her. I'll give you her number," her mother said. "And Francesca—"

"Mom," Sylvie interrupted, "thanks but no."

"What do you mean, no?" Louisa goggled at her. "You can't just turn down work. Your name is out there now, and you have to strike while the iron is hot. You need a website, a social media presence, and business cards. Do you have business cards?"

Carlos kissed his wife, effectively silencing her. Pulling back, he said, "She's got this. Stop fussing."

Louisa pinched her eyebrows together. "I'm not fussing. I'm just—"

"Fussing!" Cara and Sylvie said, then laughed.

"Fine," Louisa huffed. "But—"

Sylvie held up her hand. "No buts either. Give me your friends' names and I'll get a KBS contractor to reach out to them. That's what they do. Ron Sanchez called me and asked me to consult on some of his new builds." Her family was too busy staring to say anything, so she went on, "I think it's his way of apologizing for Dean."

Carlos looked at his wife, then at Sylvie. "And *we* need to apologize. I wish you'd told us sooner what happened. We wouldn't have blown up about you kicking in Dean's car. And we would have helped you with some money until everything got settled."

"I know that, Dad, but you were on vacation and I didn't want you to worry." If they hadn't returned home right away, there would have been a barrage of phone calls and text messages. All meant to be helpful, but she'd needed to lick her wounds and rethink her future away from her parents.

Shaking her head, Louisa squished Sylvie's cheeks together. "Mija, when you and Cara are gray-haired, I will still be worrying about you. That's what parents do."

Sylvie pried her mother's hands away and rolled her eyes. "I get that. And if I need help with something, I promise to come talk to you. Now, I need to go."

She hustled off before they could offer more advice or ask questions. Specifically about Carl. Because she didn't have answers. All she knew was that she'd let another man take advantage of her. Not her money this time, but her heart. Unable to bear the pity in his eyes or hear whatever lame words he'd planned to tell her, she'd broken off their date. He was leaving, so what was the point of seeing him again?

Straightening her spine, she drove to a house that would be coming on the market soon. Similar to Miss Jean's, it was an older three-bedroom rancher, but it had a detached dwelling unit in the large backyard. How much work needed to be done, Sylvie didn't know, and she went through her mental checklist, forcing herself to think about rodents and asbestos and mold, rather than strong arms and sweet kisses.

Half an hour later, she was up on a ladder, studying the roof of the detached dwelling unit and muttering to herself. It had initially been a tool shed, but whoever did the work had half-assed the conversion, and it was in sad shape.

She poked at a chunk of moss with the tip of her carpenter's pencil, in an attempt to dislodge it. The moss clung stubbornly to the roof before finally coming off, flying through the air and taking her pencil with it. She huffed and grumbled, but before she could take a step down the ladder, the pencil rose into the air beside her, held up by a familiar, dark brown hand.

Carl stood beneath her, silently holding the pencil. She

took it, mumbled a thank you, and went back to poking at the roof. He didn't move. She poked some more, peeking down at him every now and then. Hands in his pockets, face smooth and unperturbed, his gaze sweeping around the yard and the back of the house.

Realizing she couldn't stay there forever, she descended, the ladder shaking with each step until it stopped. Carl held the ladder steady, and each downward step brought her into his arms until she was caged between him and the metal rungs.

It was tempting to duck beneath his arm and dart away. To put distance between them like he intended to do. Instead, she twisted around and looked up at him.

"What are you doing here? I canceled our date."

He released the ladder and stepped back, leaving her feeling oddly bereft. "I know, but you didn't say why, so I came to find out. What's going on? I thought we were good?"

"When are you leaving, and why didn't you tell me?"

His brows came together. "What?"

Was he a moron? Did he think she was a moron? "Alaska. Remember? You recommended Ingrid take the marketing job so you could go to Alaska."

Anger sparked off her in waves as he continued to look at her like he didn't know what she was talking about. The hurt and frustration from the last couple of days bubbled to the surface. "You could have told me. Instead, you kiss me stupid, making me think we have something. We could be something. I was going to clean out a drawer for you for when you wanted to stay the night. I stocked up on that godawful brown sauce you put on everything. But no. I find out from Ingrid.

"She's ecstatic, by the way, and really is a perfect fit for the job, so thank you for thinking of her. She's made a PowerPoint about the direction she wants KBS to go in. But—"

Carl wrapped her in his arms and covered her mouth with his own. Licking at the seams. Demanding entrance. She told her body not to react, but it wouldn't listen. Her hands went up to cling to the back of his neck, her body molded against his, and her lips opened in welcome as tears pooled in her eyes. The goodbye kiss was perfect and would no doubt ruin her for any future kisses.

Pulling back, Carl cradled her head against his shoulder, rubbing his other hand up and down her spine. She breathed him in and sighed, memorizing the sound of his heartbeat and the solidness that surrounded her. Knowing that she'd need those memories to keep her going in the lonely nights ahead of her. She should have known it was too good to last. After the disaster with Dean, Carl was too perfect. Okay, his repertoire of things he could cook was limited, and he had never watched *Gilded Age*, but those were things that could be overcome. Living thousands of miles away couldn't.

Sylvie wasn't built for long-distance relationships. Besides, he hadn't asked. She was a good time while he'd been stuck in Keeney, and that was all. Well, she wasn't going to cling. If he wanted to kiss her again, she'd let him. If he wanted to bump uglies again, she'd do that too. Because God knows he was good at sex. Deciding that she could handle another orgasm or two and then say goodbye without a scene, she pushed against his chest.

It moved. And then again, like a minor earthquake was going through him.

She threw his arms off and glared. "Are you laughing at me?"

"No," he choked out, then pressed his lips together.

"You are!" She shoved hard, but the big, stupid man barely moved, except to wipe tears of laughter from his eyes. "It's not funny. I was going to let you give me one more orgasm before you left, but screw that noise. You can go now."

She pointed to the driveway. "Goodbye. It's been fun."

Carl captured her hands and held them against his chest. "Babe, stop. I didn't mean to laugh, but you worked yourself up into quite the tizzy." He kissed her forehead, then pressed his lips against the ridge between her eyebrows until it smoothed out. "I'm not leaving," he said.

"You're not?"

He shook his head and looked down at her. "No."

"But…you didn't take the job at KBS. I thought—"

"That I would leave the best thing that's ever happened to me? The best person who's ever happened to me? No. I'd be good at marketing, but it's not what I want to do. These last few months have made me realize I'd rather build things myself than sell something for others to build with. I'm going to stay with KBS, but as a contractor."

"You are?" Sylvie stared up at him, hope bubbling up inside her.

"I am." He kissed her nose. "I'm also going to approach a business to see if they're interested in taking on a partner. Someone who can provide an extra pair of hands, construction skills, and a little bit of cash so they don't have to work three jobs to finance their dream."

He looked at her expectantly, but Sylvie was still processing the fact that he was staying and not focusing on his words. Carl sighed, turned her around, and pointed at the house.

"You don't need someone to tell you that the patio needs to be replaced or the door is too narrow. You've got the smarts and vision to see those things yourself. You need someone to have your back and share the workload. And someone to bounce ideas off of, to be your sounding board. That's the job I'm applying for."

She turned back around to stare up at him. "Really?" she squeaked.

"Really." His gaze softened, and he cupped her face. "What you are doing with these houses is amazing. And I hope you'd like to share that with me. Gram gave me some money that I'd like to invest in your business. We'll go to a lawyer to draw up a contract and set everything up nice and legal."

He named a sum that made her eyes bug out.

"I could stop doing the drywall jobs," she murmured.

He nodded.

"I could up my bid on houses."

He nodded again.

"I could finish the houses more quickly."

"Is that a yes?"

"And you want to do this with me?" She covered his mouth before he could answer. "I mean, *with me*. You're choosing me." She held her breath, waiting for the conditions and clauses to appear. Did she want a business partner who was equally passionate about building accessible homes? Absolutely. More than that, though, she wanted Carl.

"I'm a lot." She blew out a breath that made the straggly hair around her face flutter, and pointed at her worn work boots and stained T-shirt. "I'm coarse and blunt and quick-tempered and forget to do laundry half the time."

Carl pulled the hair tie from her braid and loosened it, running his fingers through the strands, tugging gently at her scalp in the best massage ever.

"On the other hand, you'll never go hungry because I have access to the best restaurant in town."

He kneaded the back of her neck and smoothed his hands over her shoulders.

"And I have an awesome, top-of-the-line bed with plenty of room to share."

"With me," he said, his gaze boring into hers. "Only me."

"Only you—" The words were barely out before his mouth descended to claim hers. He grabbed her behind and lifted her, wrapping her legs around his waist while turning to back her against the wall of the DDU. Caught up in the delicious feel of his tongue in her mouth and his hands on her thighs, everything disappeared except Carl. The stiffness went out of her spine as the tension that had clung to her melted away, and she sank into the moment, feeling his strength surrounding her and supporting her, and knowing he wanted her and only her. She poured her heart and soul into the kiss, wishing she had the words to tell him, and hoping he understood the depth of her feelings for him.

"He-hem,"

They pulled apart to find a woman in a pantsuit staring at them. "I'm here to show Sylvie Santiago the house. Is that you?"

"Yes!"

Carl lowered her to the ground, and Sylvie fished through her tool belt to give the woman her business card.

The woman studied it, smiled, and looked expectantly at Carl.

"Right! This is Carl Ryder. He's my…partner." She beamed up at him.

Carl took the woman's extended hand. "And fiancé," he added.

The woman smiled. "Great. I don't have a key to the back door, so we'll have to go around front."

"Fiancé?" Sylvie whispered to Carl as they followed her.

"Yeah. If you'll have me." He dug a worn, velvet box out of his pocket and opened it.

Sylvie stared at the simple gold band inset with a sizable diamond, then up at Carl. His Adam's apple bobbed as he swallowed, staring back. "It was Gram's. If it's not okay, we can get something else. Whatever you want."

The box jiggled in Carl's trembling hand, the diamond winking at her in the sunlight. He always seemed so sure of things that his nervousness made her sigh, and she cupped his cheek in one hand. "It's perfect. I love it."

"Are you coming? I need to…" The woman trailed off, her frown turning into a smile. "Did he just propose?"

Gazing at the man who saw her flaws, yet wanted her anyway, Sylvie nodded.

"And you accepted?"

Sylvie nodded again as Carl kissed the palm of her hand.

"That's awesome."

Sylvie and Carl continued to stare at each other, grinning like fools, the ring box held out between them.

The woman came closer and waggled her phone. "If you like, I can take a video while you put the ring on her finger?"

"I look like crap," Sylvie said, holding out her hand as Carl took the ring out of the box.

Carl shook his head. "You look fabulous." He slid the ring onto her finger and pulled her close. "I love you, Sylvie Santiago," he whispered.

"I love you too, Carl Ryder," she whispered back, her heart so full she thought it would burst.

"That was lovely." The woman lowered her phone and sniffled. "But if you don't mind, can we look at the house now?"

"Yeah." One hand holding Carl's, Sylvie held the other up, admiring the ring as they entered the house. Together.

Worth The Risk
(A sneak peek)

Half her mind tuned in to the audiobook playing on her phone, Iris dusted the many items that filled the shelving unit in her living room. Nestled among the books, candles, and tchotchkes were a collection of framed photographs, old and new, candid and formal. She picked up the picture of her and Darryl cutting their wedding cake, dusted it, and moved on to the next one. It seemed that the most recent additions were all wedding pictures: Vincent and Hilary, Pastor Andy and Joseph, Tomas and Fiona, and finally, Marcia and Ali. In their group photograph, the happy couple were flanked by Vincent and Hilary, Iris, who'd been Marcia's attendant, and Tal, Ali's brother, who served as best man.

It was hard to tell whose smile was bigger in the picture—Marcia's or Ali's. No, maybe Vincent's. Pleased that his mother had finally tied the knot with the man who'd been besotted with her for more than two decades. Iris had watched from a ringside seat as Marcia slowly allowed Ali into her life. Iris returned the photo to its place and stood back, smiling at all the images of happy couples.

She moved on to dust the television and coffee table, thinking about the next item on her to-do list: hopefully renting out the suite on the upper floor of her house. Sylvie had moved out a few weeks ago, after buying a house she intended to renovate and flip. She'd told Iris that if everything went well, she and Carl would be finished in six months and ready to move on to the next one.

That kind of nomadic lifestyle boggled Iris's mind. She had lived in her home for almost forty years and hoped to remain in it for another twenty. But if living out of a suitcase while creating homes for others made Sylvie happy, more power to her. The girl had drive and enthusiasm for days, all of it bolstered by Carl's steady presence and support.

Iris and her late husband had had that same partnership. Most people assumed Darryl was the driving force behind Keeney Building Supply, but they would be wrong. It had been easier for a man to move about the business world decades ago, so Darryl was the face of KBS. But when it came time to make decisions, he deferred to Iris. It had been a good partnership and a good marriage.

The only cloud that dimmed her memories was their son, Eddie. He'd been released from jail after serving four years and had sent her a blistering letter accusing her of ruining his life. Then demanded money. Iris had almost complied. Instead, she'd shared the letter with her therapist, cried over her son for what she hoped was the last time, and burned the letter. She hadn't heard from Eddie since.

Movement in the backyard drew her attention to Ingrid. The young woman who had taken over Marcia's role as marketing director of KBS and resided in the tiny house was dressed in shorts and a tank top, stretching out her long legs.

"Going for a run?" Iris called from her doorway.

Ingrid grimaced. "More like a shuffle. Snails and slugs move faster than I do. If I'm not back in an hour, send out a search party."

"Will do," Iris replied. "The people who will be looking at the suite should be here by then."

"Oh, right. A young family?"

"A father and son." Iris wasn't sure of the boy's exact age, but imagined skateboards, basketballs, and other kid para-phernalia left at the foot of the stairs. The idea didn't bother her at all. She liked the energy children brought with them.

Waving, Ingrid moved into a slow jog as she reached the long driveway, earbuds in place and wearing a look of grim determination.

Iris popped in her own earbuds, pocketed her phone, and continued listening to a psychological thriller while attending to the many containers of flowers on her patio.

The heroine in the book wasn't terribly bright. *Everyone* knows that when the power goes out in a thunderstorm, you don't go down into the creepy basement by yourself. Yeesh! Iris was considering not finishing the book, but someone in her Bible study group had recommended it, and Iris didn't want to hurt the woman's feelings. She'd slog through it, maybe up the playback speed to get through it faster.

Just as the heroine's flashlight blinked out, a shadow fell over Iris. She gasped and staggered back.

"I am so sorry," a man said, holding out a placating hand.

Iris blew out a breath and removed her earbuds. "You scared me."

"I am so sorry," he repeated, his face scrunched up in chagrin. "I didn't mean to startle you."

"It's fine," Iris said. Focusing on the man, she tilted her head to the side, knowing they'd met before. "You're Tal!"

"I am," he replied. "Vitale Russo, Ali's brother." At her look of confusion, he added, "Same mother. Different father."

Iris bobbed her head. "And you're interested in the suite? For you and your son?" Just how old would this child be? Had Tal fathered a child when he should have been applying for Social Security? And where was the mother?

"Benjamin. Yes. He'll be joining us shortly," he replied. As the best man at Ali's wedding, Tal had worn a charcoal grey three-piece suit, a white dress shirt, and a tie in the same burgundy red as Iris's dress had been. Today he wore neatly pressed khaki slacks, a sage green polo shirt, and polished loafers. Unlike his brother, he had a full head of salt and pepper hair and only the slightest of paunches on his lean frame.

He was exceedingly attractive, and Iris became acutely aware of her own appearance: baggy jeans, a baggy sweater, and battered sneakers. However, if she raced into her house to raid her closet, whatever she came out with would look very similar. Despite Marcia's many offers to help her update her wardrobe, Iris couldn't be bothered. Clean and comfortable was all she needed.

And Tal Russo didn't seem to care. He smiled at her, as if he were delighted to see her. "I didn't know you were the leasing agent," he said.

"Not exactly," Iris replied. "This is my home. I live in the lower level and rent out both the tiny house and the upper level."

Tal stepped back to sweep his gaze over the house and

around the yard. "You have a beautiful property. Do you do all the work yourself?"

"Not anymore. My tenant" —she gestured at the tiny house in the corner of the yard—"takes care of mowing the lawn while I look after the flowers."

"And you do that well," he said, gesturing at a large pot overflowing with geraniums, petunias, and coleus. "I seem to recall Ali telling me you'd done the flowers for the wedding. Is that correct?"

She bobbed her head. "Not by myself, but yes. I did work on them." Memories of the wedding reception flooded her brain. Specifically, turning Tal down when he'd asked her to dance. Her response had been automatic, and gracious man that he was, he hadn't pushed. A part of her wished he had. It was the same part that kicked herself as she'd watched Tal dance with Marcia and Hilary, her feet tapping along with the music. After each dance, he'd return to sit beside her and chat, but didn't ask her again.

"Let me wash up and I'll show you the suite." Iris hustled inside to splash water on her face in the bathroom. She fluffed up her thinning gray hair and considered applying lipstick. Instead, she stuck her tongue out at the woman in the mirror, straightened her shoulders, and went back outside to where Tal was plucking dead petunia blossoms from one of the containers.

"Sorry," he said, looking guilty. "I know it encourages them to bloom again." He dropped the dead blossoms into her compost bucket and dusted off his hands. "If this works out," —he tilted his head up—"I might put some flower boxes on the railing and fill them with herbs."

"You cook?" she inquired as they climbed the stairs to the second level. She pictured Tal preparing gourmet meals and possibly inviting her to join him. She'd provide the wine and dessert, and they'd sit on the deck in the evening sun. It was a lovely thought.

"When I can. I often travel for work, and it's nice to putter in the kitchen when I'm home."

"What do you do?"

"I'm self-employed. Well, actually, Benjamin works with me. We're a two-man operation." He pulled out his wallet and handed her a heavy, embossed business card that read "Rossi & Rossi Consulting." The other side had his name and contact information. "He does most of the legwork these days, which is nice. I'm happy to spend time in the office."

She unlocked the door, and he held it open, gesturing for her to enter before him. Standing to the side of the door, she watched Tal move around the kitchen, making admiring noises that pleased her immensely. She'd worked closely with Vincent on the design that was both functional and attractive, and she hadn't skimped on the appliances. Tal went to check out the bedrooms and emerged looking quite pleased.

"One of the smaller bedrooms will work nicely as an office," he said. "I assume there's WIFI access?"

Iris nodded. "You work from home?"

"Yes. Will that be a problem?" Tal replied. "I'd rather not lease an office space that would rarely get used."

"It's not a problem," she said quickly. "It's just...I was expecting a young father and a little boy."

"And you're getting a cranky old man and his equally cranky adult son, instead." Tal's eyes twinkled.

Iris laughed. "A perfect match for the cranky old lady who lives downstairs." Heat started creeping up her neck before she'd finished the sentence. It only got worse when Tal laughed.

"I don't know what's taking Benjamin so long, but I'm happy to sign the paperwork without him," Tal said, looking at his watch. "It's not like he's going to be here all that often, anyway."

"Sounds good." Iris wanted to squeal with delight.

Instead, she led the way to her apartment, leaving Tal in the living room while she retrieved the leasing agreement.

He was studying the photographs when she returned and indicated the group photo from Marcia and Ali's wedding. "That was a great day, wasn't it? I can't believe Ali waited so long before finally asking Marcia."

Before Iris could respond, Ingrid's limping form caught her attention, and she hurried outside. "What happened?"

Both of Ingrid's knees were scraped, and she was picking gravel out of the heel of one hand. "Some dumbass on a bicycle was riding on the wrong side of the trail and hit me. Idiot," she replied, looking disgusted.

"How far away were you? Do you need me to take you to Urgent Care? How can I help?" Questions tumbled over themselves as she took Ingrid by the elbow and guided her to a chair on the patio. "Let me get the first aid kit. Do you want some water?"

Wincing, Ingrid lowered herself into the chair. "Water would be great, thanks. Urgent Care isn't necessary. It's just bruises and scrapes."

She looked inquiringly at Tal, hovering behind Iris's shoulder. Iris made the introductions, saying, "This is our new tenant. We're just waiting for his son to—"

"I told you to wait for me!" A man in cycling gear dismounted from a bike and dropped it on the grass before stalking over to confront Ingrid.

"Why? I'm fine," Ingrid went rigid and snapped. "What were you gonna do anyway? Walk me home?"

"No! Yes…something like that," the man sputtered, frustration and anger radiating from his taut frame. "I certainly wasn't going to leave you lying on the ground."

Iris got between the arguing pair and wagged a finger in the man's face. "Don't you raise your voice at Ingrid. You're the one who hit her! You have no right to be angry."

The man blinked down at Iris like he was just realizing

there was an audience and snapped his mouth shut, looking even more frustrated. Then he glanced over Iris's shoulder and groaned. "Hi, Dad. Is this the property you wanted to rent?"

For more about this and other upcoming stories, go to www.lynnehancockpearson.com to join her newsletter. You can unsubscribe at any time.

Reviews are like a warm hug, consider leaving one to let other readers know you enjoyed *Fabulously Flawed* and guide them to my books.

ALSO BY LYNNE HANCOCK PEARSON

PLANNERS & DREAMERS SERIES

Grand Gestures

Jane will grit her teeth and smile at the snobby and suspicious CFO if it means landing the contract. But she won't put on a dress and definitely not heels.

Fraudulent Trust

How was Delia supposed to know she needed to support herself? That's what trust funds are for.

Holiday Headaches

Sid and Connie are practically strangers but they could be roommates. What could possibly go wrong?

KEENEY BUILDS SERIES

#HotAndHandy

Everyone in town loves the handsome handyman. Everyone except his new neighbor.

Perfectly Polished

He made good on his promise to call. She refused to answer.

ABOUT THE AUTHOR

Lynne Hancock Pearson writes kissing books: fun, flirty, feel-good fiction that simmers at a low heat. Stories of people finding their way, even if it takes a while to get there. She lives near Seattle with her finicky felines, towering offspring, and long-suffering husband. She is a left-handed middle child who grew up in the Great White North and is a proud member of the Métis Nation of Canada.

www.ingramcontent.com/pod-product-compliance
Lightning Source LLC
Chambersburg PA
CBHW060310310726
48976CB00007B/2278